(2)

GW01086003

The Dream

The Dream

by Avner Gold

CIS

C.I.S. Publications Division
Lakewood, New Jersey

Published by:
C.I.S. Publications Division
674 Eighth Street
Lakewood, N J 08701
Tel: (201)367-7858

Typography by:
C.I.S. Graphics
674 Eighth Street
Lakewood, N J 08701

Typeset by:
Shami Reinman
Devora Oberman
Rivky Deutsch

Printed and Bound by:
Gross Bothers, Inc.
3125 Summit Avenue
Union City, N J 07087

Contents

Editor's Note

AMONG THE EARLY VOLUMES of the popular *Ruach Ami Series, The Dream* has emerged as a singular favorite of young readers, both as an enjoyable book to read and as a script for school and camp plays. While no new chapters have been created for this revised and expanded edition, the plot and the characterizations have been significantly modified and enhanced. The "dream" around which the plot revolves has been much more elaborately developed and several important elements have been incorporated into it.

In addition, a new cover illustration, of a style consistent with the cover illustrations of the other volumes of the *Ruach Ami Series,* was specially commissioned for this edition. Unlike the cover illustration of the first edition of *The Dream* which portrayed some of the images of the "dream," the new cover illustration depicts an undisturbed landscape of Pulichev as it lies nestled between steep mountain slopes alongside the banks of the Gryzdna River. One of the reasons for this decision has been to give the readers of the *Ruach Ami Series* a "street map" of Pulichev, so to speak, which can be used in conjunction with all the books. This is of particular importance in *The Year of the Sword,* the third volume of the series, where the layout of Pulichev plays a crucial role in the story, and it also plays an important role in *The Purple Ring,* the sixth volume of the series.

Other modifications in this new edition of *The Dream* have been in the nature of subtraction rather than addition. In the first edition, the very first part of the book was essentially a recapitulation of the story of *The Promised Child* for the edification of readers unfamiliar with the newly published *Ruach Ami Series*. Since then, however, the *Ruach Ami Series* has become a popular mainstay of quality literature for young, and not so young, Jewish readers, and recapitulation of story lines was no longer deemed necessary. The first edition of *The Dream* also described the transitional period in Shloime Pulichever's life subsequent to the climactic events of *The Promised Child*. This description does not appear in the new edition of *The Dream* since it has already been incorporated into the revised and expanded edition of *The Promised Child*.

The historical setting of *The Dream* is in the southern provinces of the Kingdom of Poland in the year 5405 (1645), a time of unrest and upheaval in the central part of the European continent. The Thirty Years' War had been dragging on since 5378 (1618), and the German states lay devastated. The war, which was to end as an inconclusive stalemate with the Treaty of Westphalia in 5408 (1648), solidified the power of the Catholic Church and stemmed the tide of the Protestant Reformation. The renewed power of the Church reached out to the frontiers of Christendom with the Jesuit Order as the spearhead. This caused great problems in Poland, a devoutly Catholic country with an immense Greek Orthodox population in the Ukraine, its most prized possession. The tension between the Catholic and Greek Orthodox elements grew almost unbearable as the year 5408 (1648) drew near.

At the same time, a seed of even greater disaster was germinating in Poland. The Polish overlords of the Ukraine acquired vast estates across the entire territory. Often, the Ukrainian estates of a Polish nobleman would include hundreds of villages and many thousands of serfs, but although he drained off all their wealth, years could pass without him setting foot on them. To manage the estates both in his presence and in his absence, the Polish nobleman needed townsmen to whom he could rent the various leases. Very often, these townsmen were Jewish people, who at that time constituted the bulk of the Polish middle class. Therefore, the nobles and the Jews were associated in the eyes of the Ukrainian peasant and equally despised.

In 5408 (1648) matters would come to a head, and the Ukrainians would vent their rage on their Polish overlords, the Catholic clergy and the Jews, as described in *The Year of the Sword*, the third volume of the series.

In *The Dream,* the kettle has not yet come to a boil, but it is growing rapidly hotter as the tensions in the Ukraine spread into the rest of the Kingdom of Poland. As the story unfolds, the tension poses a harrowing threat to the safety of the Jewish community of Pulichev. The Pulichever family responds to the threat with courage and faith in the *Ribono Shel Olam,* and in the end, disaster is averted. But the volcanic forces of destruction continue to percolate underneath the surface. In the next volume of the series, *The Year of the Sword,* these forces are unleashed

Y.Y.R.
Lakewood
5746 (1986)

The Dream

The Black Shadow · 1

S HLOIME PULICHEVER WALKED ALONG the banks of the Prosna River below the tiny hamlet of Wielkowicz holding the unopened letter in his hands. Presently, he sat down on an overturned log and looked at the letter once again. It was from his father, the famous Reb Mendel Pulichever, *Rav* of Pulichev in eastern Galicia and world renowned Torah authority. The letter had arrived earlier in the day, but Shloime had waited for a moment of solitude before he opened it. He glanced back over his shoulder to make sure he was alone.

Wielkowicz was just a stone's throw away. The entire hamlet consisted of one small group of picturesque cottages clustered at the foot of a craggy hill. High on the crest of the hill stood the ruins of a medieval castle, its crumbling towers painted red by the rays of the setting sun. To the south stretched the narrow valley through which the river came tumbling out of the dark green hills. To the north lay the broad plain through which the river made its leisurely way to join the distant Warta River and continue on to Poznan. There was no sign of movement as far as the eye could see.

My father chose well, thought Shloime. Wielkowicz is indeed a place of beauty and serenity, a place for private thoughts and private pursuits.

Shloime waited a few moments more just to savor the anticipation for a little while longer, then he opened the letter. A worried frown appeared on his brow as he read his father's small, tight script, and his feeling of uneasiness grew as he read the letter several more times. Something was wrong at home in

15

Pulichev. He could sense it.

It had been nearly two years since Shloime had seen his father and mother. For a brief moment, Shloime's thoughts flashed back to the long dark period earlier in his life when he had been separated from his parents. He had been abducted as a small child and brought up in a monastery in the belief that he was the orphan child of a peasant family, eventually becoming a bishop. His parents had been heartbroken, and he himself had always felt an unexplained emptiness and yearning. Then, just three years ago, he had been reunited with his parents at the age of thirty-one in an amazing turn of events that had thwarted an evil scheme against the Jews of Krakow.

Shloime's thoughts turned to the first year of his reunion with his parents. It had been pure bliss, but he had not caught up in his Jewish learning as much as he should have. The demands on Reb Mendel's time were simply too great for him to be able to give his son the proper attention. One evening, Reb Mendel and the Rebbetzin had both sat down with Shloime and tearfully suggested that he study for two years with his father's uncle Reb Yomtov Luria, an exceptional *Talmid Chacham* who lived by himself in the faraway village of Wielkowicz. It had been a difficult decision for all of them.

Reb Yomtov was a delight. He was a mild, unassuming man, with little interest in anything but his *sefarim*, and he was so excited to see Shloime he didn't know what to do first. He had come out to greet his guest in his long tattered caftan and his ancient black hat, which many years of ingrained dust had turned into a murky gray. Obviously bursting with curiosity about Shloime and his family, he asked no questions. He fed the weary traveller and showed him to the room they would share.

The following day, Reb Yomtov took Shloime for a walk along the river. They talked a little about the past and a lot about the future. Together they devised a program for the next two years. They learned together for only a short while that first day; Reb Yomtov insisted that Shloime go to sleep early and get some more rest. That night the sounds of weeping awoke Shloime.

Through half-closed eyes he saw Reb Yomtov sitting on the floor in a corner of the room, saying *Tikun Chatzos* and weeping over the destruction of Yerushalayim over fifteen hundred years before.

Reb Yomtov had proved himself a wonderful teacher. His knowledge of the Torah and all things Jewish was encyclopedic, and his patience was inexhaustible. The responsibility he had assumed seemed to have unlocked a hidden store of energy and reinvigorated the old man. He had devoted himself tirelessly to Shloime. He had asked provocative questions and guided him to discover the answers for himself. With time, it had become easier and easier to do so, and more rewarding. Shloime was dazzled by the beauty and the endless intricacy of the Torah as it unfolded before his eyes.

The time had passed quickly. There were very few people in Wielkowicz and none whom he could logically befriend, but Shloime did not mind. All his waking hours were spent in Reb Yomtov's company, and he never tired of it. Even in everyday conversation Reb Yomtov's sharp insights and salty comments never failed to delight him. Sometimes Shloime felt that Reb Mendel had sent him to Wielkowicz to learn more than just the written words of the Torah.

During all this time, Shloime's only contact with his parents had been through the exchange of letters. Reb Mendel was invariably interested in his progress, offering some of his own thoughts on the particular *Gemara* Shloime was learning; his mother invariably inquired about his health and comfort. And both of them wrote eagerly of the day he would return and settle down to a productive Jewish life. Shloime read the letters from home many times.

But this last letter from home was different from the rest. Shloime read it over and over trying to sense his father's thoughts. True, the inquiries were substantially the same, but the tone was unmistakably different. There was no enthusiasm, no vitality; it was almost mechanical. And why hadn't his mother also written? What was going on in Pulichev?

A light touch on his shoulder startled him out of his reverie, and he looked up to see the kind face of Reb Yomtov. Immediately, he stood up.

"Didn't you hear me calling?" asked Reb Yomtov.

Shloime shook his head.

"I'm afraid I didn't hear you," he said. "My thoughts were far away."

"What's on your mind, Shloime? You seem worried."

Shloime tapped the letter in his hand.

"It's this letter from my father," he said.

"Ribono Shel Olam!" exclaimed Reb Yomtov, clutching at his heart. "What has happened in Pulichev? What misfortune has befallen us?"

"Oh, it is probably nothing," Shloime hurriedly reassured him. "My father doesn't mention anything out of the ordinary in the letter. It's just an uneasy feeling I got from reading it, as if my father's mind was distracted by some deep concern when he was writing."

"I'm sure it is nothing, my dear Shloimele," said Reb Yomtov, obviously relieved. "He was probably busy with a difficult *Halachic* problem."

"But why didn't my mother write?"

Reb Yomtov shrugged.

"There is probably some simple explanation for that, too," he said. "The letter carrier probably arrived when your mother was out of the house and your father was busy with something else. Not to waste the opportunity, your father dashed off a letter to you without giving it the proper care. You will see, his next letter will be more cheerful."

"I hope you're right," said Shloime.

"You will see, Shloime, there is no need to worry," said Reb Yomtov and stood up. "Come, let us go back to the house. I will make us some tea. How does that sound to you?"

Shloime smiled and stood up, too.

"It sounds very good," he said. "Only, I will be the one to make us the tea."

"You know, Shloime," said Reb Yomtov as they walked back to the house. "You remind me very much of my brother-in-law, Reb Shloime Pulichever, your father's father, the one after whom you are named. You always worry a lot. My wife, may she have a *lichtige Gan Eden,* used to tell me that he was also like that, even when they were children. Believe me, Shloime, it is not good. It is much better not to worry. Come, let us learn something new for a few hours. That will set your mind at ease."

The hours of learning did indeed set Shloime's mind at ease, but as soon as he went to bed, his earlier worries returned. For a long while, he lay quietly in the silent darkness, brooding about his father's letter. Then, he fell into a troubled sleep and began to dream.

He dreamed that he had come to Reb Yomtov and told him he was going home. His parents needed him. He had only come for two years in the first place anyway, and the two years were almost over. But Reb Yomtov was not cooperative. You are making too much out of one letter, he claimed. Wait a while, he insisted. But Shloime refused and started to leave. Reb Yomtov grabbed his arm and wouldn't let go. Finally, Shloime pulled his arm free and fled into the hills.

He ran stumbling through the wooded hills, crashing into trees that loomed in front of him and calling out as he ran, "Mother! Father!"

His voice echoed through the hills and came back to him, as if to mock him.

"Ribono Shel Olam!" he cried out at the top of his lungs. "Help me! Please help me!"

Darkness fell, but Shloime continued to run. His legs ached with unbearable fatigue, but he kept on running until he could run no more. Exhausted, he sat down under a tree and tried to sleep, but sleep refused to come.

The tall dark shapes all around indicated that he was in a forest. Soon, the night became cold, and he began to shiver. A chill wind moaned through the spectral trees and rustled their invisible leaves. The moaning grew louder and louder until a horrible dread gripped Shloime's trembling heart. He covered his ears to shut out the awful moaning sound and prayed that morning would come quickly. After an interminably long time, he took his hands off his ears. The moaning had stopped. In its place, a deathly silence had descended on the forest.

Shloime had never experienced a silence such as this in all his life. It was a total, utter silence, as if the whole world had ceased to exist or as if he had become totally deaf. No sound of the wind or the forest animals or movement of any sort. Except for just one sound. The sound of his own heart beating thunderously in his chest.

Shloime tried to calm himself but couldn't. The beating of his heart grew louder and louder and louder still until it seemed to fill up the entire forest. He tried to put his hands over his ears to shut out the awful beating sounds, but it didn't help. The sounds came from within.

Shloime could take no more, and a shrill scream escaped from his lips. Instantly, the awful sounds ceased and the peaceful sounds of the sleeping forest returned. He sighed deeply and closed his eyes. A powerful drowsiness gripped him, and he let the merciful sleep overcome him.

Suddenly, he sensed he was not alone. In an instant, the drowsiness was completely dispelled. He sat forward and peered into the impenetrable gloom of the forest, but he saw nothing. Presently, he heard a soft scratching sound to his right. He spun around and rose into a crouch.

A dark amorphous shape had appeared some distance away. None of its features were visible, only a pair of brilliantly gleaming amber eyes. Shloime remained frozen in his place, transfixed by fright.

"What are you?" he breathed.

"What do you want in this forest?" replied a hollow voice. "Why have you disturbed my sleep?"

"Who are you?" cried Shloime. "What are you?"

"It is better you do not know. What is your name?"

"Shloime Pulichever."

"Why were you running through this forest?"

"I am deeply sorry if I have disturbed your sleep. I am on my way home to Pulichev. I think something is wrong, and I must go home."

"Pulichev is very far away. Running on foot, it will take you many weeks to get there."

"I must go. I must go. It is very important."

"And what will you do when you get there?"

"I don't know. I will do something."

"Beware of the short one, Shloime Pulichever."

"What do you mean?"

"Just what I say. Beware of the short one. Remember what I am telling you. You will one day understand."

"What is happening in Pulichev? You seem to know. Please tell me. I must know. It is very important."

"Go to sleep now, Shloime Pulichever. You can sleep in peace. In the morning, you may continue your running. Remember what I have told you."

"But what —" He did not complete the sentence. The dark shape had vanished.

Shloime closed his eyes once again, and he fell into a strange, otherworldly kind of sleep. After what seemed like a brief instant, he opened his eyes and it was morning.

Immediately, he resumed his running, but inexplicably, he was now running more swiftly than the fleetest deer. He leaped from hill to hill, scrambled over mountains and darted through forests.

At noon, he climbed to the top of the last hill and there was Pulichev lying in the valley below him. He stopped to catch his breath and survey the scene below him. Pulichev seemed as lovely and peaceful as ever. Had he been wrong? Was everything actually all right? Had it all been only his imagination?

All of a sudden, a huge black shadow detached itself from the facing hillside and started to make its way down into the valley. Wrapped in a hooded black cloak and towering over the trees, the giant figure glided silently down the hillside towards

Pulichev. Shloime's heart pounded violently as he ran screaming down the twisting roadway into Pulichev. He waved his arms furiously and shouted to the people to beware, but no one took notice of him. They didn't pay him any attention at all; it was as if he wasn't even there. He tried to grab some of the people by their lapels, but they just slipped through his fingers.

The giant figure had now entered Pulichev and was walking right down the center of the main street. The people milling about the street didn't seem to notice anything out of the ordinary. But they must have sensed *something,* because they all moved aside instinctively to make way for its passage.

Frantic with desperation, Shloime jumped on the giant figure, beating at it with his flailing fists, but it just brushed him aside as if he were an insignificant fly. Shloime scrambled to his feet just in time to see the black shadow turning the corner into the street where Reb Mendel and the Rebbetzin lived. With a cry of rage, Shloime set off in pursuit. He caught up to it near Reb Mendel's house. Strangely, the black shadow had stopped and was watching the house carefully. Shloime couldn't think of anything to do, so he also stopped and waited to see what would happen. The black shadow glanced briefly at Shloime then turned its attention back to the house.

Presently, Reb Mendel came out of the house and looked up and down the street. It was obvious that he saw neither Shloime nor the black shadow as they stood just several paces away. Then, he stepped into the street and started walking directly at the black shadow. The shadowy figure radiated hatred toward Reb Mendel, but Reb Mendel kept coming. At the last moment, the black shadow stepped aside. Unlike the other people of Pulichev, Reb Mendel had not sensed the presence of the black shadow at all.

The black shadow waited until Reb Mendel disappeared from sight, then it approached the house. With one swipe of its huge hand it swept aside the entire front wall of the house, exposing the rooms inside. And there stood the Rebbetzin in the kitchen busy with her cooking and completely unaware of this monstrous figure that loomed over her. She didn't even seem to notice that the front wall had been ripped away.

The black shadow bent down and began to reach out towards the Rebbetzin. The aura of malevolence that emanated from it made Shloime quake with dread.

Although Shloime knew he was powerless against the black shadow he couldn't just stand by idly. Screaming at the top of his lungs to get his mother's attention he sprang forward, but his way was blocked. Directly in front of him a whole group of people had appeared. Everywhere he turned someone else appeared to block his way until they formed a tight circle around him. At first he didn't recognize these people, but then he did. They were some of the churchmen he had known during the lost years. He pleaded to be let through, but instead, they laughed in his face. Their mocking laughter grew louder and louder until the street rocked with the sounds. Surely this will catch my mother's attention, he thought desperately. But she didn't seem to hear anything at all.

Shloime reached for his last ounce of strength. With a sudden burst he forced his way through the ring of laughing churchmen and ran into the kitchen. He threw himself as a shield in front of his mother and turned to face the black shadow. The black shadow had bent down to position its head in front of the kitchen. Its eyes were like two smoldering coals as they peered out at Shloime from the shadows of its hood.

The laughing churchmen had now vanished. The Rebbetzin continued with her cooking as if nothing was happening. Only Shloime and the black shadow were aware of each other's presence. Shloime could sense the black shadow's anger building, but he refused to budge.

Abruptly, it drew itself to its full height and let out a mighty roar like a deafening clap of thunder. Then it reached into the exposed kitchen, grabbed Shloime by the left arm and yanked him into the air. It lifted Shloime high above the rooftops of Pulichev and began to shake him. And shake him. And shake him.

"Shloime, Shloime, wake up!" Reb Yomtov was saying as he

shook Shloime's left arm. "What's going on? Why are you screaming?"

Shloime saw Reb Yomtov only faintly; in his mind he was still in the grips of the huge, black-cloaked figure. But the anxious look on the kindly old man's face slowly released Shloime from his terrible nightmare. He awoke with a start, trembling and disoriented. Then the details of the nightmarish scene flooded back into his mind, and he shuddered.

"Shloime, are you all right?" asked Reb Yomtov.

"I've just had a very strange dream, but I'm fine. I'm sorry if I startled you."

"It doesn't matter, as long as you're all right. Let's still try to get some sleep."

In the morning, Shloime told Reb Yomtov the entire dream as best as he remembered it. Reb Yomtov listened intently without comment until Shloime had finished, except for a brief smile at the part where he had held on tightly to Shloime's arm refusing to let him leave.

"So what do you think? What does the dream mean?" asked Shloime when he had finished.

"Dreams are strange things, you know," replied Reb Yomtov. "Not all dreams have significance. And even those that do still have some chaff, some nonsense. You received this letter from your father that disturbed you, and your concern expressed itself in the form of a foreboding dream. You felt that I would be against your going back at this point, hence the scene where I try to hold you back. The danger in your dream centers around your mother because she didn't write the last time, probably for some perfectly innocent reason."

"How about the strange figure in the forest and its warning about the short one? How about the hatred the black shadow radiated towards my father? How about the fact that my father did not sense the black shadow's presence at all while the other people at least felt it, even if they didn't actually see it? How about the circle of laughing churchmen?"

Reb Yomtov nodded. "That may be significant. On the other

hand, it may have quite an ordinary explanation, although none comes to mind immediately."

"Then you really are against my returning to Pulichev?"

Reb Yomtov sighed heavily.

"No, my dear Shloimele, I am not," he said. "These last two years have been a gift from heaven to an old man. You've been the son I had never had and had long despaired of having. But your place is by your father's side, not mine. You came to Wielkowicz to learn Torah with peace of mind, and I think I've been quite a good *melamed*. But one thing your dream shows for sure. Your mind is no longer here in Wielkowicz; it is in Pulichev. I'm afraid my usefulness has come to an end. Who knows if I shall ever see you again?"

Tears glistened on the old man's wrinkled cheeks and streaked his sparse white beard. Shloime put his arms around his beloved uncle and hugged him.

"I can never even begin to thank you for what you've done for me. I hope we shall yet see each other again. I will always remember you and think of you. Wherever I go you will be with me. Always."

"*Ay*, memories," mused Reb Yomtov. "We must all live with our memories. In the end, that is all we have left. Our memories, and the little bit of Torah and *mitzvos* we manage to gather in the short time we spend here in this world."

The old man fell silent, lost in distant thoughts.

"I want you to remember, Shloimele, that you have a great responsibility. All those years you lost were necessary so that you could defeat the evil schemes of Zbigniew Mzlateslavski, the mad priest of Pulichev, at that fateful debate in Krakow. But now, you must return to your original destiny. It is not too late for you to carry on in the illustrious tradition of the Pulichever family. You have a gifted mind and a profound understanding of the Torah, and you must not be satisfied with an ordinary life. You have the responsibility and the ability to become a great *Talmid Chacham*. I know you will do it and that I will have had a part in it."

Shloime remained silent, his eyes moist with tears.

"So, Shloimele," said Reb Yomtov, pulling himself out of his pensive mood. "You must go back to Pulichev as soon as you can. And remember your dream. If there is indeed trouble in Pulichev, then the dream was surely a message from Heaven. A warning certainly, and perhaps also the key to finding the answers you will seek. And also remember, dear Shloimele, things are not always as they seem. Never forget that."

Two days later, Shloime bade Reb Yomtov farewell and boarded a wagon travelling from Poznan to Krakow that passed through Wielkowicz to drop off a cobbler. The old man remained standing in the road, leaning on his cane, long after the wagon had disappeared from sight.

Elisha Ringel · 2

F LOCKS OF MIGRATING GEESE flew high above the wagon
as it rumbled south through the Malopolska Hills
towards Krakow, its half-rotted wood creaking and groaning
under the weight of its load. The prodigious struggles climbing
up the hills were followed by wild, hair-raising descents down
the opposite slopes. The driver, a bad-tempered peasant who was
half-drunk most of the time, whipped his scrawny horses
mercilessly.

The passengers were an assorted lot. Facing Shloime were
three Jewish musicians who had been summoned from Krakow
all the way to Kalisz to play at the wedding of a nobleman. Beside
him sat an old couple who constantly mumbled to each other and
ignored everyone else. Sitting in the back by himself with his feet
dangling over the end was a dark, tiny young man who looked at
Shloime speculatively every once in a while. It was not until the
second day that he spoke to Shloime.

"You look very familiar," he said. "Do I know you from
somewhere? Do you live around here?"

"No. I'm afraid I don't. I was just visiting a relative in
Wielkowicz."

"Well, maybe I saw you somewhere else. My name is Elisha
Ringel. What's yours?"

"Shloime Pulichever."

"Any relation to Reb Mendel Pulichever?"

"I'm his son."

Recognition flashed in Elisha Ringel's eyes.

"Of course!" he exclaimed. "I saw you in Krakow three years

27

ago. No wonder I didn't recognize you. You looked a little different then, all dressed up as a bishop. You really humiliated that priest, the one with the long name I always forget. No one spoke of anything else for months."

"Well, I would rather not speak about it if you don't mind," said Shloime. "That is a period in my life I would much rather forget."

Elisha looked crestfallen.

"There were so many rumors at the time," he said. "Couldn't you at least tell me which ones are true?"

"Perhaps some other time," said Shloime with a tone of finality that belied his words. "Why don't you tell me something about yourself? From where do you come?"

"I'm just a wanderer. I come from nowhere."

"You must come from somewhere."

"I've lived here and there. Nothing permanent."

"Don't you have any family?"

"No."

"What do you do?"

"I do nothing. I just travel from place to place and look around. I'm twenty-eight years old, and I haven't a zloty to my name. Now you know everything about me."

"But from what do you live?"

"Some odd jobs. I don't need much."

"Where are you headed?"

"Wherever this wagon will take me."

"It's taking you to Krakow."

"True. But there I'll catch one going somewhere else."

"Where?"

"I don't know yet."

"I see."

"Do you really see?" asked Elisha.

"No, I don't suppose I do," replied Shloime.

Elisha shrugged.

"It doesn't matter anyway," he said. "Well, it seems neither of us wants to talk much about himself. Why don't you come sit beside me on the tail of the wagon and we can talk of something else?"

They made an odd pair sitting together, their feet dangling over the tail of the wagon, the one tall, fair and reserved, the other short, dark and effervescent. But once they warmed to each other they spent hours talking about anything and everything. Elisha was impressed by Shloime's vast knowledge, Shloime by Elisha's sharp wit.

The next day brought a steady downpour. All day they travelled through the driving rain, trying to protect themselves as best they could but getting soaked to the skin nevertheless. They made hardly any progress through the mud-choked road. By nightfall they were still in the open country nowhere near any of the roadside inns. They camped alongside the road, overturning the wagon and going to sleep under it.

Morning brought a break in the weather, and they were able to continue their journey. Shloime and Elisha stared bleary-eyed at the soggy landscape. Elisha had developed a hacking cough. They were both hungry and exhausted. They travelled in a sort of dazed silence. It was a very subdued group that stopped at a roadside inn that night.

They started out very early the next day. It was already Thursday, and they would have to hurry if they hoped to reach Krakow before the nightfall of the following day. Otherwise, they would have to spend *Shabbos* on the road.

That afternoon they stopped to rest on the crest of a high hill with a spectacular view. In the distance they could make out the Vistula River. They would reach it by midmorning tomorrow and follow it east into Krakow.

"Poland is quite a beautiful country, wouldn't you say?" remarked Elisha.

"Yes, it is a good country."

"Unfortunately, it is not good for Jews."

"What are you talking about? Look about you," Shloime said as he jabbed his finger in every direction. "Poznan. Breslau. Lodz. Warsaw. Krakow. The Pulichev region. The Ukraine. Kiev.

Wherever you go in the Kingdom of Poland there are thriving Jewish communities. Things have been good for the Jewish people in Poland. The king and the nobles have always protected us. They will continue to protect us."

"How could you say that after what happened in Krakow?"

"That was just an isolated incident. Things like that will happen here and there every once in a while, but not as a rule. After all, it is in their own interest to protect us. They need us. We are the financiers and the tradespeople. Who else would perform these services for them? It is beneath the nobility and even the country squires to do it themselves, and the common Polish people are serfs."

"Yes, this is quite true. But there are pressures building in Poland. How long do you think they will be able to keep up their feudal system? How long do you think a handful of powerful families can concentrate all the wealth of Poland in their own hands and keep millions of people in poverty?"

"They've done it for centuries."

"You listen to me, Shloime Pulichever. I've been all over the Kingdom of Poland and the Grand Duchy of Lithuania. There is big trouble brewing. The Catholic Church of Poland is going to clash with the Orthodox Church of the East. Who do you think will get caught in the middle? Not the Jews? The Cossacks are probably going to revolt in the Ukraine. Who do you think will be the first to feel their sword? Not the Jews? Believe me, if Poland is thrown into turmoil the Jews will be the first to suffer."

The strong feeling with which Elisha spoke took Shloime by surprise. Elisha's face had become flushed; his breath came in shallow gasps. He was seized by a fit of coughing that brought tears to his eyes. For the first time, Shloime noticed Elisha's sallow complexion, the brown blotches on his face, the sharp bones clearly outlined against the tightly stretched skin.

"Elisha, my friend," Shloime said. "Since you are not going anywhere in particular and have no attachments and responsibilities to anyone, why don't you come with me to Pulichev for a while?"

"Why?" asked Elisha suspiciously.

"Well, obviously your health isn't very good. It doesn't look like you've been taking care of yourself. Come with me to Pulichev. You can continue on your wanderings when you've regained your strength. In the meantime, we'll be company for each other."

Elisha thought for a moment and said, "Why not? I've never been to Pulichev. I suppose I might find it interesting."

"I have to warn you, though. Pulichev is not Krakow."

"But it's not Wielkowicz either, is it?"

"No, it isn't," laughed Shloime. "I think you'll like it."

They spent Thursday night in a small hostel owned by a Jewish family. The food was kosher, and for the first time that week they were able to eat a hot meal.

While he was eating, Shloime's thoughts turned to Krakow. He had not passed through Krakow on the way to Wielkowicz. Reb Mendel had suggested that he go instead through Lublin and Radom to receive the blessings of Reb Henach Altman and Reb Uri Berliner. Both of these holy men were extremely old and had since died. Shloime was happy that he had taken his father's advice. But tomorrow he would see Krakow once again. He wondered if the Jewish community had changed much over the past three years. He looked forward to seeing his father's old friend Chaim Tomashov.

A harsh rasping sound interrupted Shloime's thoughts. He looked up to see Elisha doubled over and coughing uncontrollably. His food lay on the table untouched. His face was a sickly color. Shloime ran to his friend and grabbed him about the shoulders.

"Elisha," he said softly. "Let me help you to your room. I think you should lie down for a while. I'll tell them to save your food. You can eat later when you feel better."

But Elisha didn't feel better later. His fever rose sharply, and he fell into a fitful sleep. Shloime did not sleep in a bed that night. He dozed in a chair by Elisha's bedside. Whenever Elisha groaned Shloime was instantly awake. Several times through the night he held Elisha's head and poured a little water through his parched lips. Elisha seemed to improve a bit just as the sun stretched its tentative fingers over the horizon, and Shloime dozed off.

It seemed as if he had been asleep for only a few minutes when the innkeeper woke him.

"Reb Yid," he whispered to Shloime so as not to waken Elisha. "It's seven o'clock. Your wagon will be leaving in about an hour. You still have to *daven* and eat."

"My friend here is very sick. Do you have any medicines?"

"My wife knows something about herbs. You go on to Krakow. We'll take care of him here. Don't worry about him. He'll be fine."

"No!" came Elisha's hoarse whisper from the bed. He had propped himself up on an elbow and was looking about for his clothing. "I am not staying here. I'm coming to Krakow."

"But you're too sick to travel," protested Shloime. "I'll tell you what. I'll stay here with you, and when you get better we'll both go on to Krakow."

"No!" insisted Elisha as he struggled to his feet and began to get dressed. "You are going to Krakow, Shloime Pulichev, and I am coming with you."

Stopover in Krakow · 3

ELISHA HAD TO BE HELPED to the wagon by Shloime and the innkeeper. Shloime took some old bedding from the inn and laid it out in the well of the wagon. He offered to pay for the bedding, but the innkeeper wouldn't hear of it. Together, they made Elisha as comfortable as possible and covered him. Shloime sat down next to him.

The driver cracked his whip, and they lurched forward. After about an hour, they came to a smooth stretch of road. Elisha fell asleep, and Shloime dozed off as well.

When Shloime awoke they were travelling along the north bank of the Vistula on the main road into Krakow. The other passengers were all dozing, and the driver was muttering under his breath. Shloime looked up at the sun. It had already moved into the western sky; *Shabbos* was fast approaching.

Krakow loomed before them suddenly as they rounded the last bend in the river. The large walls of the old city towered over the smaller walls of the Jewish section of Kasimierz at the southern tip of the city. Only selected Jews were allowed into the old walled city, and only to do business, not to live there. The road entered Krakow through Kasimierz. They arrived at Chaim Tomashov's doorstep an hour before *Shabbos*.

Their unexpected arrival caused great excitement in the Tomashov household. A servant was immediately dispatched to summon the Jewish physician who lived in the next street. Chaim Tomashov himself ran to prepare rooms for them while his wife brought food from the kitchen. Servants were sent to bring in their bags and to bring them fresh suits of clothing. Elisha was

33

filled with steaming chicken soup, bundled into a warm feather-bed and covered with an eiderdown quilt. By then the physician had arrived to examine Elisha. He prescribed lots of rest and warm nourishment and left some medicine for him to take. Elisha grimaced at the awful smell but swallowed it anyway. In a short while, his cough subsided, and he fell into a deep sleep.

Chaim Tomashov and Shloime went to *shul* for *Kabbalas Shabbos* and *Maariv.* Once they turned into the Breit Gass, the "broad street" of Kasimierz, they found themselves surrounded by hundreds and hundreds of men streaming towards the seven main *shuls* of Krakow.

Chaim Tomashov had grown old and usually *davened* in the nearby Rema Shul, named after the great Reb Moshe Isserles, the revered *Rav* of Krakow a century before. This *Shabbos*, however, he took his guest to the Alte Shul, a magnificent Gothic structure almost two hundred and fifty years old in which fully a thousand people came to *daven.* The sound of a thousand voices joined together in the sweet melodies of *Lechah Dodi* brought tears of joy to Shloime's eyes.

The gatherings in the *Bais Hamikdash* in ancient Yerushalayim must have been something like this, he thought. What a special place this Krakow was!

After two years in tiny Wielkowicz, *Shabbos* in Krakow was an overwhelming experience. Shloime hardly slept that *Shabbos*, although he certainly could have used the sleep. When he wasn't talking to Chaim Tomashov he walked about Kasimierz thirstily drinking in all the sights. He visited the *shuls*, met the *Rabbonim* and listened to their *drashos* and *shiurim*. There was a vitality and excitement in the city not to be found in placid village life. Shloime was convinced that the Jewish community of Poland was going to become increasingly concentrated in large cities. Krakow represented the future.

After *Shabbos*, the physician returned to examine Elisha. The patient was much improved but would still need a few days of bed rest, he said, and it would be at least a week before he could travel. Elisha wanted Shloime to leave right away; he would follow later. But Shloime insisted on waiting for him. If he left without him, he explained, Elisha would not follow him.

Elisha's recovery was rapid. He had a surprisingly strong constitution for such a frail, tiny man. By the end of the week he was roaming Krakow together with Shloime.

Friday morning, Elisha suggested they go see the old walled city. Shloime agreed, though not without some misgivings. Dressed as peasants, they entered by the Florian's Gate and wandered about the old city. They visited "Jewish Street" and the "Gate of the Jews." They went to see the ruins of the old *shul* in Spigalski Street, deserted since Jews had been excluded from the old walled city in 1495, but dared not enter for fear of being discovered. From there they found their way to the Ring-Platz and saw the old town hall. Making their way to the southwest of the city they came upon the Stanislaw cathedral, in whose majestic halls the kings of Poland were traditionally crowned. Shloime had been here almost fifteen years before to witness the coronation of King Wladislaus IV. He remembered it well and described it to Elisha in detail.

As he was talking, a young Franciscan monk approached them.

"Hey, you two," he called. "Come with me."

"Where are you taking us?" asked Shloime.

"Don't ask any questions. Just come."

"I'm sorry," said Elisha. "We can't come. Our wives are waiting for us in the marketplace. They'll have our heads if we come late."

"And I'll have your heads if you give me any more of your back talk," snapped the monk. "You are keeping your betters waiting. You certainly have a lot of insolence for a pair of miserable peasants. Follow me!"

The monk spun on his heel and headed off across the cathedral plaza. Shloime and Elisha exchanged worried glances and followed the monk.

Across the plaza, there was a small park, consisting of marble benches arranged around an ornate marble fountain. The monk led them to a group of churchmen sitting on one of these benches. Shloime's blood drained from his face as he recognized them.

"So, you haven't forgotten us entirely, have you, Gregor? Or should we call you by a different name now?" said Bronislaw Kowalski, the Bishop of Fabiansk. He turned to one of his companions who had a baffled look on his face. "Are you wondering who this is, Father Danieuz?"

"Indeed, I am, Father Bronislaw," replied the other priest. "Who is this peasant?"

"Then by all means let me make the introductions," said the Bishop of Fabiansk. "Danieuz Kroidski, our esteemed Rector of the Jagiellonian University. This peasant here was once called Gregor Tal."

"The Bishop of Lubianewicz?"

"One and the same," said the Bishop of Fabiansk. He turned to the third member of the group. "Isn't that so, Father Jan?"

"Yes, it is," said Jan Bilutsa, the Bishop of Malonavka. "I would recognize him anywhere."

"So, Gregor, what should we call you now?"

"My Jewish name, the name I was given at birth, is Shloime. My name is Shloime Pulichever."

"Never mind," interrupted Danieuz Kroidski. "We'll just call him Jew. I have an account to settle with you, Jew. I was looking forward to that debate three years ago. I was going to record it myself. I was even prepared to write a commentary. You cheated us."

"I had to save my people," said Shloime. "It was the only way."

"Listen here, Tal. It is still not too late for you to return to the church. In view of the circumstances, these past three years can be excused. Repudiate the Jews and embrace Christianity once again. A man of your scholarship can always have a post at the University. Think of what a sensation it would be. Many other Jews would probably follow your example. You would get much credit for returning to the church after having tasted life as a Jew. They might even make you a bishop again. Yes! That is a capital idea! I will help you become a bishop again. I give you my word."

"I must respectfully decline your offer," Shloime said, the sarcasm unmistakable. "I have indeed tasted Jewish life, and I prefer it."

"I will tolerate no insolence from you, Jew," hissed Kroidski, his face crimson with fury. "I will have you thrown into prison for trespassing in the old city."

"Calm yourself, Father Danieuz," said Bronislaw Kowalski. "He has only been a Jew for a short while. In time, he will learn to speak with proper respect to his betters."

"A few nights in prison would teach him very quickly," fumed Kroidski.

"No, Father Danieuz," said Bronislaw Kowalski. "Better to let him go now. If we have him arrested the Jews will run screaming to the King saying that we are using his trespassing only as a pretext to make trouble for the Jews. They will also claim that we are really trying to coerce him to return to the church. Do not underestimate these Jews, Father Danieuz. They are a crafty lot. Let us bide our time. If he doesn't learn his place he will sooner or later destroy himself. Isn't that so, Father Jan? Don't you agree?"

"Certainly, certainly," said the Bishop of Malonavka.

"Come, gentlemen," said Bronislaw Kowalski, rising from the bench. "Let us continue our walk. This company is beginning to irritate me."

Danieuz Kroidski rose to accompany Kowalski, but Jan Bilutsa remained seated.

"You continue your walk without me," he said. "I'm still weary. I want to sit here a while longer."

Since they had not been dismissed, Shloime and Elisha remained standing in the little park as the two priests walked off. Jan Bilutsa paid them no attention until the two priests disappeared around a corner.

"You shouldn't have come here, Pulichever," he finally said. "It was unwise."

Shloime remained silent.

"Who is your friend?" asked Bilutsa.

Elisha had been totally ignored until this point.

"He is Elisha Ringel, my close friend. He is travelling with me to Pulichev."

"Where are you from?" Bilutsa asked Elisha.

"I'm from Lvov."

"I would ask you to have a seat," he said, addressing both of them, "but it would be unseemly for peasants to sit with a bishop in public."

Shloime breathed a sigh of relief. He had always liked Bilutsa. He had found him fair and compassionate. Apparently, he had remained a friend in spite of what had happened.

"We've known each other for a very long time," said the Bishop of Malonavka. "In a strange way, I still think of us as friends. After all, your father's position is equivalent to that of a bishop. You haven't really changed stations, just religions."

"Unless you feel that to be a Jew automatically puts one on a lower station," said Shloime ironically.

"No, I don't feel that way. You believe what you want to believe, and I'll believe what I want to believe. Who am I to tell you what to believe?"

"It's strange to hear a bishop speaking like that," said Shloime cautiously.

"Is it really? Isn't that the way you felt when you were a bishop yourself?"

"Yes, it was," said Shloime. "I'm certainly glad to hear you feel this way, too."

"You know, Pulichever, there is unrest in Poland. Especially in the Ukraine where the influence of the Russian czar grows stronger by the day. The Cossacks are in turmoil. You Jews had better be careful."

"What can we do?"

"Nothing, really. Besides leaving."

"And where would we go?"

Jan Bilutsa nodded.

"Indeed, where can all the Jews of Poland run to hide?" he

mused. He paused before going on. "It is a difficult thing, indeed. But, listen to me, Pulichever. Pulichev is not far from Malonavka at all, you know. If you have any trouble let me know about it. I might be able to help you. But, you must understand, that it is highly unlikely that I will be able to do anything. After all, most churchmen do not share my liberal views. You cannot expect me to jeopardize my position in the church simply to save the Jews."

"Of course not," said Shloime hastily. "Your kind offer is most welcome. I will keep it in strictest confidence. I will not avail myself of it except in the most extreme circumstances."

"Very good. By the way, about that debate, I have to admit that I was also looking forward to it. We all ended up looking a bit foolish, you know. Especially that old priest who set up the whole thing, that Father Zbigniew Mzlateslavski. He was really humiliated. It was his downfall."

"He brought it upon himself," said Shloime. "As to the debate, you wouldn't have enjoyed it anyway. The cardinal would not have let it be a fair exchange of ideas."

"Yes, I suppose that's true," admitted Bilutsa grudgingly. "Old Szmerka was a bigot, and a senile one at that. He died last year, you know."

"No. I hadn't heard."

"Yes, he did. It's a wonder he lived this long. Stefan Provkin, who used to be Archbishop of Krutsk, was appointed in his place. Now he's Stefan Cardinal Provkin. Sounds nice, eh?"

"Yes. Jan Cardinal Bilutsa sounds quite good, too."

"Doesn't it? Well, maybe some day," said the Bishop of Malonavka, obviously uncomfortable. The conversation was getting too intimate, not the kind of conversation one had with Jews, even if one of them had once been a bishop. He stood up.

"Well, gentlemen, I shall be going," he said and walked away.

As soon he was gone Shloime and Elisha headed for the nearest gate. They did not slow down until they were back in Kasimierz.

"You know something, Shloime," Elisha said when they were back in Kasimierz. "These Kroidski and Kowalski characters, I can understand them. They show exactly what they are, rotten as it is. But this Bilutsa character, I can't figure him out."

"I used to be quite friendly with him. I got to know him very well. He's a strange man, a little confused. I suppose the best way to describe him is to say that he is a natural reactionary obsessed with the idea of being a liberal."

"I see."

"By the way, Elisha," said Shloime as they turned into the street where Chaim Tomashov lived. "I'm a little annoyed with you. When I ask you from where you've come you gave a whole slew of evasive answers. But when Bilutsa asks, you answer like a little lamb. Is that fair?"

"Do you really think I come from Lvov?"

"Don't you?"

"Of course not. I've never been there in my life."

They were both laughing as they came into the house. Chaim Tomashov greeted them warmly.

"I'm happy to see that you've both had an enjoyable morning."

"Some of it was certainly enjoyable," said Shloime.

"What do you mean?" asked Chaim Tomashov.

Shloime told him about their experience. With some help from Elisha, he managed to piece together almost the entire conversation. Chaim Tomashov's expression became very grave as he listened to the account.

"Yes, these are trying times. But *Shabbos* is coming. Let's not talk about things that bring sadness. I have some good news for you. A friend of mine, a wealthy financier, is leaving for Odessa in his private carriage Sunday morning. He will be glad to take you to Pulichev. I'm sure your parents can't wait to see you again."

"Thank you so much," said Shloime. "That is truly wonderful news, especially after the conditions on the first leg of our journey."

Chaim Tomashov smiled.

"Oh, and I almost forgot," he said. "When he drops you off in Pulichev maybe you can persuade him to spend *Shabbos* there.

It's always a problem when you're travelling, even if you have a private carriage."

"Of course," said Shloime. "We will be glad to have him for *Shabbos.*"

Their second *Shabbos* in Krakow was every bit as enjoyable as the first, only this time Elisha was able to accompany Shloime on his visits to the various *shuls*. After *Havdalah,* Chaim Tomashov asked Shloime to step into his private room.

"Well, Shloime," he began. "You're leaving tomorrow morning. It's been a pleasure having you. Come anytime. My house is your house."

"When can you come to Pulichev? We would like to return your hospitality."

"It's not likely to be soon. Give my very best to your father. Your father is the most wonderful person I know. I feel very close to him. We don't see each other too often, but we always write. In fact, I just received a letter from him ten days ago."

Chaim Tomashov paused.

"Shloime, I didn't bring this up before," he continued when Shloime remained silent, "because I felt that if you didn't say anything you probably didn't want to talk about it. But I can't let you leave without asking you. Shloime, how is your mother?"

Shloime felt as if icy fingers had touched his heart.

"What are you saying?" he finally managed to whisper.

"Hasn't your father told you?" asked Chaim Tomashov in a puzzled tone.

"What is the matter with my mother?" he asked. "Please tell me."

Chaim Tomashov sighed wearily.

"*Ay,* that I should be the bearer of bad news," he said. "Your mother is ill. Very ill."

Arrival in Pulichev · 4

ARLY THE FOLLOWING MORNING Shloime and Elisha left Krakow in Moshe Prochovnik's luxurious carriage. Chaim Tomashov had risen before daybreak to see them off in the blustery autumn weather. Shloime was visibly distraught by the unexpected news of his mother's illness, and Chaim Tomashov had tried to reassure him.

"You must have *bitachon* in Hashem, my dear Shloime," he had said. "I remember many years ago saying similar words to your great father, Reb Mendel, when he thought he had lost you. Be strong, Shloime. Your parents need your strength."

"Yes, you are right," Shloime had replied and bidden him farewell. But it was easier to say the words than to feel them.

Moshe Prochovnik, an aristocratic, elderly man, was a polite and gracious host, but he was preoccupied most of the time. He spent his time familiarizing himself with the accounts of the business ventures in Odessa that were awaiting his inspection. Whenever he was not doing paperwork he took out a small, leatherbound *Mishnayos* and learned from it. Sometimes, he would just sit there with his eyes closed and softly say *Tehillim* by heart, chanting the holy words with reverence and emotion.

Shloime and Elisha enjoyed watching the countryside that passed by the carriage window. At Shloime's insistence, they also learned together in one of Moshe Prochovnik's *Gemaras*. Although Elisha was not entirely ignorant, Shloime had to spend much time pointing out some of the most basic concepts of *Talmudic* learning. Elisha listened with interest, obviously impressed by Shloime's clever observations and the chains of distinctive Talmudic reasoning.

At some of these sessions, Moshe Prochovnik would interrupt whatever he was doing and quietly listen to the sometimes heated arguments of the two young men. They in turn honored him by asking him to read aloud from the *Mishnayos* and to explain it to them. It was an altogether satisfactory arrangement.

They made good time, reaching Kolbitz by *Shabbos*. Two days out of Kolbitz, they were attacked by bandits.

The bandits had apparently been lying in ambush, waiting for a carriage which looked promising. Moshe Prochovnik's luxurious carriage looked promising.

The attack came on a long and lonely stretch of road hemmed in on both sides by dense forest. The bandits appeared in the middle of the road, the leader holding his hand up in a signal for them to stop. However, instead of stopping the driver spurred his horses on to their fullest speed. The bandits scattered before the hurtling carriage, but as soon as the carriage had passed through, they set off in hot pursuit.

Moshe Prochovnik's driver cracked his whip again and again over the heads of the powerful horses bringing them to a headlong gallop, but the fully loaded carriage was simply too heavy. The horses tired, and the gap between the carriage and the bandits grew steadily narrower. The worst fears of the travellers were about to be realized; it was unlikely that any of them would be left alive.

Shloime and Moshe Prochovnik prepared for the end, but Elisha pulled his bag from under the seat and rummaged about inside. With a cry of triumph, he brought forth a small burlap sack. He reached into the sack and with an impish grin on his face he pulled out a handful of long iron nails.

"Do not despair, my friends," he said. "We will come through this danger safely. You will see."

He opened the window in the carriage door. The thunderous roar of the pursuing bandits was deafening.

"Now, hold on to my legs tightly," he said.

Elisha clambered halfway out the window as Shloime and Moshe Prochovnik grabbed his legs. Elisha crooked one arm around the doorpost of the carriage holding the sack of his nails in his hand. With his other hand he reached into the sack and began strewing handfuls of nails on the road behind them.

Almost immediately, one of the bandits' horses reared up in terror as it stepped on a nail. The rider was thrown clear and landed on the roadside. Some of the other horses panicked at the sight of the rearing horse, and the bandits were thrown into confusion. Only two of the bandits continued in pursuit, but they too soon abandoned the chase. Elisha threw one more handful of nails into the road for good measure, then he climbed back into the carriage.

"You saved our lives, young man," said Moshe Prochovnik. "How can I ever thank you?"

Elisha shrugged.

"It was nothing," he said nonchalantly. "Just a small trick I once learned from a travelling companion."

Two days later, they arrived in Pulichev.

Excitement was written all over Reb Mendel's face as he rushed out to meet the carriage. When its passengers stepped down he gave *Shalom Aleichem* to the elderly man first, then to the unfamiliar Elisha. Only then did he embrace his beloved son.

After Shloime had introduced his two guests to Reb Mendel and arranged for their accommodations, Shloime took his bags and joined his father in the privacy of the study.

"How is Mother?" Shloime asked as soon as they were alone.

"Your mother is very ill, Shloime," replied Reb Mendel. "She is too weak to get out of bed. We've consulted all the physicians in Pulichev and the surrounding district, but no one has been able to diagnose her illness."

"Did you call in any of the *goyische* physicians?" asked Shloime.

"You know that the best physicians in Poland are Jewish," said Reb Mendel. "But we left no stone unturned. We consulted with all the best *goyische* physicians. We even called in a monk from the monastery at Prestokow, upon the recommendation of Karol Triefak, the local priest, but he couldn't help us either."

"What exactly is wrong with her?"

"She suffers nausea and stomach cramps. She can't keep food down. She gets dizzy spells and sometimes feels like she is choking. Nothing helps her. She just keeps getting weaker and weaker."

"There must be something we can do," said Shloime, a note of desperation creeping into his voice.

"Believe me," said Reb Mendel. "We've tried everything."

"But if she doesn't eat, how does she get nourishment?" asked Shloime. "Without food she will just waste away."

"One of the physicians prescribed a porridge of dried cereals mixed with grated apples that had been left out to turn brown and an assortment of herbs. He also suggested bananas, but they are difficult to find. We keep a jar of this mixture in her room. She takes a few spoonfuls several times a day. It seems to be getting her by."

"Are we totally helpless then?" asked Shloime. "There must be something we can do."

"Your mother needs a real *refuah shelaimah,* Shloime," said Reb Mendel in a grave voice. "It seems there is no course left to us but to put ourselves completely in the Hands of the *Ribono Shel Olam.* We have exhausted every remedy. The only remedy we have not exhausted is the remedy of *tefillah,* because it is inexhaustible. We must *daven* to the *Ribono Shel Olam.* And we must have *bitachon* and accept his decrees with humility and without question."

Shloime nodded.

"Yes, Father," he said bowing to the wisdom of his father's words.

Suddenly, he realized he had been thinking only of his mother, not his father.

"And how about you yourself, Father?" he asked. "How have you been managing?"

"I don't need anything for myself," replied Reb Mendel. "I do whatever I can for your mother. Some of the neighboring women come by to bathe her. Come, you must be weary. We can talk some more later. You can go lie down."

"First, I would like to see Mother," said Shloime.

"Naturally," said Reb Mendel. "She is sleeping right now, and I don't want to disturb her. You go lie down. I will call as soon as she gets up. Go upstairs. I will ask Kalman Kalb to take your bags up to your room."

"Who is Kalman Kalb?"

Reb Mendel stared at him blankly for a brief moment. Then, he smiled and tapped his forehead.

"For a moment, I forgot how long you've been away, my dear Shloime," he said. "Kalman Kalb has been here for a while, but he came after you left. It's hard for me to describe him. He's a pitiable old man. He cannot speak, and he doesn't always understand when you talk to him, but he's not exactly an idiot either. He came to Pulichev some months after you left, ragged and penniless. Your mother showed him kindness. She fed him and let him stay about the house. It doesn't seem as if too many people have shown him kindness. Your mother apparently reached the tormented soul that hides somewhere in poor Kalman Kalb. Maybe the *zchus* of her kindness will help her overcome her illness."

"Does this Kalman Kalb live here?" asked Shloime. "I mean, here in this house."

"Not exactly, Shloime," said Reb Mendel with a mildly embarrassed look. "He has taken a kind of liking to me, and he stays close to me most of the time. He eats most of his meals here sitting on the floor outside my study. Sometimes, he goes out in the evening when the streets are empty and roams all over Pulichev. Otherwise, he stays away from other people. At first, the children used to be frightened of him, but everyone's gotten used to him. Most people pay him no mind."

"And where does he sleep?"

"He sleeps in the *shul*."

"In *shul*? Why?"

"That's where he wants to sleep. We gave up trying to get him to sleep elsewhere. He just lies down on the last bench and goes to sleep. Your mother sent along some pillows for him."

"I am quite curious to meet this Kalman Kalb," said Shloime. "I don't think I'll go lie down. I'll wait for Mother to get up."

"Very well," said Reb Mendel. "She should be up soon anyway. In the meantime, tell me about your journey."

"I will be happy to tell you about the journey," said Shloime. "Many interesting things happened, but first I would like to tell you about a dream I had in Wielkowicz."

Reb Mendel listened with rapt attention as Shloime told him of the shadowy black figure and how it had been intent on harming his mother. For the better part of an hour, they discussed the dream and the significance of dreams in general, then they were interrupted by a knock on the door.

"Come in," Reb Mendel called out.

The door opened, and Kalman Kalb came in.

Shloime was totally unprepared for the sight that confronted him. He had never seen such a grotesque person. Kalman Kalb's large body was hunched over almost double as he stood before them. His face was hideously disfigured by a network of livid scars. His eyes stared out suspiciously from under drooping lids. His beard was a group of tufts of brittle gray hairs scattered over his jaw. He wore an often-patched brown suit and a heavy wool cap stretched tightly over his skull.

Shloime stood frozen, but Reb Mendel hurried over to the old man.

"Kalman, my good friend!" he exclaimed, placing an arm about the shoulders of the disfigured old man. "I want you to meet my son. He has just come back home after being away for two years."

Kalman Kalb grunted.

"That's the best you can expect from him, Shloime," said Reb Mendel with a shrug. "I'm not even sure if he understood me."

"Do you think Mother is awake?" asked Shloime.

"She is probably awake by now. Go right up," replied Reb

Mendel. He pointed to Shloime's luggage. "Kalman, please help Shloime with his bags."

Shloime and Kalman Kalb walked up the stairs together. At the top of the stairs, Shloime took Kalman Kalb's hand in his and shook it.

"It was nice meeting you, Kalman," he said. "I hope we can be friends."

Kalman Kalb grunted and walked away. Shloime tapped lightly on the door to his mother's room.

"Come in," said a feeble voice.

Shloime entered. There was a candle burning in the room, but it was that twilight time of the late afternoon when candles are ineffective and the sunlight leaves only shadows.

"Mother," he said. "It's me. I've come home."

The Rebbetzin's eyes fluttered open. When she saw Shloime she started to weep. Finally, the sobs subsided.

"Oh, Shloimele, Shloimele," she said, dabbing at her eyes. "I'm so glad to see you. How grateful I am to the *Ribono Shel Olam* for letting me see you again!"

Shloime pulled a chair over to the bed and sat down.

"Mother, you must get well," he said. "With Hashem's help, we'll find the cause of your illness and the cure. But you must be strong. Do you hear me? You must be strong."

She tried to reply but no words came out. Instead she squeezed Shloime's hand and closed her eyes. Shloime stood up.

"I think you should try to get some rest now," he said. "The excitement seems to have tired you."

The Rebbetzin nodded weakly. She motioned silently towards a table upon which there stood a pitcher of water and a covered jar.

"Can I get you a drink of water?"

The Rebbetzin nodded but continued to motion.

"Something to eat?"

The Rebbetzin nodded again.

Shloime opened the jar. It contained the porridge the physician had prescribed. The herbs gave it a pungent, though not unpleasant, odor. Shloime poured some water into a glass and scooped out a spoonful of the porridge. He fed the Rebbetzin and gave her to drink. Then he waited until she fell asleep. Only then did he walk quietly out of the room. Kalman Kalb was sitting at the bottom of the stairs. He stared at Shloime as he passed by, but he made no sound. Not even a grunt.

Ephraim Surkis · 5

FAMILIAR SIGHTS GREETED SHLOIME as he went for a stroll later that evening. Pulichev had not changed much in the two years of his absence. He would have liked to walk about some more, but he was too weary from the journey and returned home.

Entering the house, Shloime heard the sounds of loud conversation coming from his father's study. The door was wide open, and he went in. Reb Mendel was in deep conversation with Moshe Prochovnik, Elisha Ringel and an unfamiliar young man who rose and came towards him with his hand outstretched.

"Shalom Aleichem," said the young man, grasping Shloime's hand in both of his and shaking it vigorously. "I'm Ephraim Surkis. I'm honored to meet you."

"The honor is mine," said Shloime without any sign of recognition.

"Ephraim is your cousin by marriage, Shloime," explained Reb Mendel. "His wife Bracha is your mother's niece. They live in Pulichev now."

"Oh, Mother wrote me about you," Shloime said to Ephraim Surkis. "I just didn't recognize the name right away. You used to live in Zamosc, didn't you?"

"That's exactly right," Ephraim cried out, obviously delighted that Shloime had indeed heard of him. Then he said in a graver tone, "We are all praying for your mother's recovery. I am sure the *Ribono Shel Olam* will not let our *tefillos* go unanswered."

"Sit down, Shloime," said Reb Mendel. "Reb Moshe Prochovnik has been telling us about the Ukraine. He's passing through there on the way to Odessa. You were saying, Reb Moshe?"

"I was just saying that there is going to be a lot of trouble there for the Jews," said the elderly gentleman. "The Ukraine is not really a natural part of the Kingdom of Poland. The people are different; the language is different; the climate is different; the Orthodox Church is very strong there. Russia has designs on the Ukraine and is doing its best to stir up trouble. And the Cossacks are a violent people. Who knows what they would do if aroused?"

"But why should they attack the Jews?" asked Shloime.

"Because we are a convenient target. We are the middle class of Poland, and we are Jews. If the peasants want to win concessions from the ruling aristocracy by showing their rage, what better and safer way to do so than by attacking Jews?"

"Do you think this is going to happen?"

"It's already happening. Have you ever heard of Bogdan Chmielnicki?"

"No. I haven't."

"He is a powerful Ukrainian Cossack. He has engineered small insurrections here and there. I hear that he's been negotiating an alliance with the Tatars of the Crimea. If he is successful there will be an explosion in eastern Poland."

"What can the Jews of the Ukraine do about it?"

"Why do you ask only about the Ukraine? Poland is a weak country. There is no central army; every powerful nobleman has a small, private army of his own. If the Cossacks rise they can sweep across all of Poland, not stopping until they reach the Prussian border. They will leave nothing standing."

"How soon can this happen, and what is to be done?" asked Shloime.

"I think all Jews should be ready to leave Poland if things get worse," interjected Elisha Ringel. He had been silent throughout this exchange.

"And where would you have all the Jews of Poland go?" asked Ephraim.

"Anywhere," said Elisha.

"But you can't think of a specific place, can you?" asked Ephraim. "Persecution in the west drove the Jews into Poland. Conditions to the east are even worse. And to the south we have the Turks sitting across half of Europe. Let's face it. There is nowhere to go."

"I'm not saying that we should all leave now. I'm just saying that we should be prepared to leave on short notice. We can decide at that time which direction is safest."

"What do you say, Reb Moshe?" asked Reb Mendel.

"I agree with Ephraim. You know, my family has been in Poland for many centuries. In fact, I am a direct descendant of Avraham Prochovnik."

"Are you really?" asked Shloime. "How wonderful! I should have made the connection."

"Would anyone care to enlighten me?" asked Elisha. "Who was this Avraham Prochovnik?"

"I'll be glad to," said Moshe Prochovnik. "Prochovnik is an old Polish word for merchant. The word literally means dust-covered. I suppose merchants were called dust-covered because they were always travelling. My ancestor was a merchant from Germany who was travelling through Poland some seven hundred years ago, just about the time Poland was first being organized as a state. They needed a king, but the noble families were afraid that if the king were one of their own he would become too powerful. Legend has it that they decided to elect the first foreigner who came into the country. That turned out to be none other than my ancestor. Here there are two versions. Some say that he declined the crown, and they elected the fabled King Piast instead. Others say that he accepted and served for a few weeks before he abdicated. Anyway, my ancestor settled in Poland, and we've been here ever since."

"I also have to agree with Ephraim," said Reb Mendel, joining in the debate. "An entire community of hundreds of thousands of people cannot live the way you suggest, my dear Elisha. It is not practical. Only selected individuals can follow your advice. And that leaves the problem for the majority unsolved. Reb Moshe, what do you think should be done?"

Moshe Prochovnik stroked his beard thoughtfully. "For the Jews of the Ukraine there's really nothing to do, except to prepare hiding places and pray. As for the Jews of the western provinces of Poland, everything must be done to control local tensions. Then there is a chance that if the Cossacks revolt it will not spread to these parts of Poland."

"What exactly do you mean?" asked Shloime.

"I mean that there are always some disgruntled gentiles who are troublemakers. Ordinarily, they do not present a grave danger to the entire community. But in times like these, when the whole country is like a tinderbox, anything can set it off. We must be very alert for any of these petty schemes directed against us and foil them before they get out of hand."

"That sounds reasonable," said Shloime. "Father, have we been having any trouble here in Pulichev?"

"Nothing out of the ordinary," said Reb Mendel. "What we Jews must never forget is that we are in exile. Our place is in Eretz Yisrael, with a rebuilt Yerushalayim, living in a society in which the Torah is the law. For over fifteen hundred years we have lived among the gentiles, but we have never forgotten where our true home lies. We must really be grateful to the *Ribono Shel Olam* for the hardships of exile; they do not let us forget who we are and what is required of us."

Reb Mendel suddenly stood up.

"We can continue this conversation tomorrow," he said. "Right now, I think we should all get some sleep. Some of us have come from quite a distance and must be very tired."

Reb Mendel's suggestion was eagerly accepted. Within the hour the house was silent.

Shloime awoke at the crack of dawn feeling completely refreshed. He hadn't slept that well in a very long time. It was probably a combination of the physical comfort of sleeping in his own room and the peace of mind that came with being home again.

When he came downstairs he found his father sitting in the

study with a *Chumash*. He looked up when Shloime came in, surprised to see him up so early after such a long journey. But he appreciated the company of his beloved son in the private stillness of the early morning hours.

Father and son walked together through the gray light to *daven* with the first *minyan*. As they approached the *shul*, Reb Mendel suddenly stopped.

"Shloimele, I don't have the key with me. I left it at home."

"Should we turn back?"

"No, let's go on. Maybe someone has already opened it up. I have a spare key in the *shul*. When we get in I'll give it to you. You're not as forgetful as I am."

The *shul* looked completely deserted. Shloime tried the door. It was locked. Reb Mendel started to shiver in the chilly air. It seemed they would either have to wait in the cold for someone else to come along or walk back to the house. Shloime tried the door once again, pulling hard at it in the hopes of jarring it open. But it was to no avail. The massive old doors wouldn't budge.

Shloime looked around for another means of entry. It was hopeless. The *shul* had been built like a fortress to provide security for the Jews of Pulichev. The only windows were high up and barred. Even if one could find an unlocked window and clamber up the wall to reach it, it would still be almost impossible for a man of normal size to squeeze through the bars.

They had already turned to leave when the door suddenly swung open behind them. Kalman Kalb stood in the doorway.

"Good morning, Kalman," said Reb Mendel. "Forgive us for disturbing your sleep."

Kalman Kalb grunted and stepped aside to let them pass. He then returned to his bench and went back to sleep.

"Does Kalman Kalb have a key to the *shul*?" asked Shloime.

"No, he doesn't," replied Reb Mendel. "He is always here at night when the *shul* is locked up. If he wants to go out to wander about Pulichev for an hour or so he just leaves the door unlocked till he comes back. And now, let me give you the spare key."

Reb Mendel opened the cavernous drawer in the bottom of

the *Aron Hakodesh* in which everyone kept his *tallis* and *tefillin*. He rummaged deep within the drawer, almost disappearing from sight as he groped in the deepest corners. With a cry of triumph he emerged holding the key aloft. He gave the key to Shloime and closed the drawer.

People were beginning to come in. Within a few minutes *Shacharis* had begun. The sounds of the prayers woke Kalman Kalb. He retreated to a corner of his bench and sat there watching until everyone was finished. Reb Mendel wrapped up his *tefillin*, folded his *tallis* and returned them to the deep recesses of the drawer. Then he gently took Kalman Kalb by the arm.

"Come eat breakfast, Kalman," he said.

As the three of them walked home, Shloime smiled with pride as he thought about this *tzaddik* who was his father. In spite of his great prominence and the honors which came his way, there was not a trace of vanity or arrogance in Reb Mendel. Shloime marvelled at the depth of his father's humanity and genuine compassion for even a rejected creature such as Kalman Kalb. How fortunate I am, thought Shloime, to have such a father and, yes, that my mother has these qualities as well.

A hearty greeting intruded on Shloime's thoughts. Moshe Prochovnik, Elisha Ringel and Ephraim Surkis were coming towards them. Ephraim had stopped by the house to make sure that the others would not miss the later *minyan* for *Shacharis*. Shloime liked his robust young cousin. He radiated energy and enthusiasm. He would make a kind and loyal friend and a steadfast ally.

"Father, tell me about Ephraim," said Shloime when they were back in the house.

Reb Mendel smiled.

"I can see that you like him. Everyone does. He comes from one of the most respected families of Zamosc. He married your mother's brother's daughter Bracha about nine years ago. They have four children, three boys and a girl. Ahrele, Chaim, Sender and Chanele. He sells the finest imported cloth. His silks and brocades are incredibly beautiful. He sells to royalty and the aristocracy, both here in Poland and beyond. In fact, the reason they moved to Poland is to be closer to the Hungarian border. He sells cloth to the Hungarians and the Turks as well."

"Where is his store?"

"In Pirchatka Square," said Reb Mendel. "Are you thinking of going there?"

"Yes. I thought I would drop by and get acquainted."

"That's a good idea. He will be very happy. But go towards evening when it is not so busy."

Shloime spent most of that day sitting by his mother's bedside. Late in the afternoon, Elisha joined him and they went to see Ephraim. As they entered the store they almost collided with a short, red-faced man who came storming out, muttering and shaking his fists. They hurried into the store not knowing what to expect. Ephraim stood at the counter, calmly folding a bolt of cloth.

"What did that fellow want?" asked Shloime.

Ephraim laughed.

"Did he frighten you?" he asked. "That's Roman Szczyrk. He's a blacksmith. He wanted me to give him some of my most expensive cloth in return for protecting my store."

"And what did you tell him?"

"I told him that the only one from whom he could protect me was himself, and I could do that myself."

"He seemed quite insulted."

"You needn't worry about him," said Elisha, dismissing the whole affair with a disdainful wave of the hand. "Look, I'm just about ready to close up and go home. Why don't the two of you come along and meet my family? We'll be more comfortable there anyway. I'm sure they'll be very happy to meet you."

"Sounds like a good idea," said Shloime. "Elisha?"

"Sure."

Ephraim mounted a heavy metal grating across the storefront and locked it securely in place. They stopped in a small *shul* for *Minchah* and *Maariv*. From there it was just a short walk to Ephraim's house.

Bracha Surkis could hardly contain her excitement at meeting her celebrated cousin. She ushered her guests into the cozy parlor. She brought in platters of cake and served them fragrant tea in delicate china teacups. She brought in her children, but before she had a chance to introduce them, Shloime addressed the children by their correct names. Shloime laughed at the surprised expressions on the faces of the parents. His father had told him the names only this morning, he explained.

The evening passed very pleasantly. When it was time for Shloime and Elisha to leave, Ephraim escorted them out into the street. They did not notice the shadowy figure crouching among the trees across the way. Ephraim waited until his guests were out of sight before he turned to go back. Only when the door had closed behind Ephraim did Roman Szczyrk emerge from the shadows. He glared at the house for a while. Then he vanished into the night.

Karol Triefak · 6

THE WINTER MONTHS PASSED slowly, and the Rebbetzin's condition remained unchanged. She lay in her bed, weak and pale, barely able to speak, drifting in and out of fevered slumber.

A routine developed in the Pulichever household centered around her needs. Shloime would sit with her during the morning hours when Reb Mendel received the people that came to consult with him. Reb Mendel would relieve him in the afternoons, and Shloime would go to the *shul* to learn. And as always, Kalman Kalb would sit at the bottom of the stairs waiting for Reb Mendel to emerge. He seemed to have warmed a little to Shloime, glaring at him less suspiciously than before.

Elisha Ringel found life in Pulichev enjoyable, but he was beginning to feel restless. Often, he would join Shloime in the *shul* during the afternoons. Elisha had a sharp mind and Shloime enjoyed teaching him, but very often Elisha's mind was elsewhere. He knew that he could not stay on in Pulichev indefinitely, and he was already thinking about the next place in his wanderings.

Ephraim Surkis offered Elisha a job. Since he liked to travel so much, Ephraim suggested, why not use his wanderlust to earn a living? Why not sell cloth to the nobility of distant places? Ephraim and Elisha would share the profits. Elisha was deeply touched by the offer, but he politely declined. His mind was made up; he would leave Pulichev as soon as the spring thaw set in. Shloime did convince him, however, to stay on in Pulichev until after *Pesach*.

Spring found Pulichev in a troubled mood. Reports of sporadic revolts in outlying parts of the Ukraine trickled in. Returning merchants and other travellers brought rumors of pogroms by marauding bands of Cossacks as close as the Kamenets-Podolski region.

In Pulichev itself there was a rash of inexplicable incidents. In the worst, the barn of a peasant who was a notorious Jew hater was burned to the ground. Rumors spread that the Jews had done it out of revenge, but Count Leszek Bernowiecz, the nobleman on whose vast estates Pulichev stood, sent his soldiers to protect "his" Jews, forbidding anyone to retaliate against the Jews unless their guilt could be proven.

The Jews breathed a sigh of relief, but it was premature. The following Sunday, Karol Triefak, the local priest, got up on the pulpit and accused the Jews of having burned down the barn. He knew this for a fact, said Triefak, because a messenger from Heaven had come to him and told him about it.

Triefak's fiery words whipped his parishioners into a frenzy. Armed with this "proof" and led by the blacksmith Roman Szczyrk they burst from the church and burned down a score of Jewish stores while the count's soldiers stood by. Fortunately, no Jews were injured in the outbreak of violence.

Reb Mendel and Shloime tried to keep the Rebbetzin from finding out what was going on, but even in her weakened condition, she sensed the tension and insisted that she be told everything.

"Shloimele, please tell me exactly what happened," she whispered hoarsely. "My body may be wasting away, but my mind is healthy. Don't you realize that what you're doing is worse than telling me the truth? I lie here imagining that the most horrible things are happening. If you want to help me, please tell me."

"Very well," said Shloime reluctantly.

"And promise not to keep anything from me in the future. Will you promise me that?"

"I promise it."

"Thank you," she said. "Now start from the beginning. Who

knows? I may be able to think of something helpful."

The Rebbetzin closed her eyes as he began to speak. He told her of his experiences in Krakow. He told her everything that had happened in Pulichev since his return that had any bearing on the current troubles. He even told her about meeting an infuriated Roman Szczyrk outside Ephraim's store. But he did not tell her of the dream in which she had been threatened by the black shadow.

The Rebbetzin listened intently until he finished. Then she lay quietly for a while. Only the sound of her shallow breathing punctuated the tense silence. Finally, she opened her eyes and began to weep.

"Shloimele, my dear child," she sobbed. "We waited so many years for you to be born. Then when you were taken from us we waited so many years for you to return. Then we again waited two years for you to come back from Wielkowicz. I'm happy that you went, but it was so very hard for me to let you go."

"It was hard for me too, Mother," said Shloime quietly.

"But I was hoping that now I would finally see some *nachas*. Maybe in my old age I would have the joy that other people have in their younger years. I hoped you would marry and have children, that I would live to hold my own grandchildren on my lap and sing to them as I once sang to you."

"Please don't cry, Mother," said Shloime. "Don't worry, everything will turn out well. The *Ribono Shel Olam* will take care of us, as he always has."

As soon as he had spoken, the Rebbetzin seemed to reach into an inner reservoir of strength.

"You are right, Shloime," she said. "Have you thought of any possible steps to ease the tension?"

The Rebbetzin's words reminded him of Moshe Prochovnik's advice back in the autumn months.

"We've been considering several things," he replied, "but we haven't really come up with anything good."

"Why don't you go meet with Karol Triefak?", asked the Rebbetzin. "After all, he's the one who started this whole incident with his inflammatory sermons."

"How would that help?" asked Shloime.

"I've never met Triefak, but I've always heard that he's quite harmless," said the Rebbetzin. "My impression was always that Triefak is a simple fellow. A bit of a fool. Did you ever think that someone might have put him up to this mischief? If you can find out who is behind it you will have solved half the problem."

"You know, Mother," said Shloime. "I think you may be right. We all underestimated you. We should have sought your advice right from the start."

Shloime wasted no time. The following day, accompanied by Elisha, he went to confront the priest.

Karol Triefak lived alone on the edge of Pulichev in a house overlooking the apple orchards of the lower valley. As Shloime and Elisha approached they thought for a moment that they had been given wrong directions. They heard the unmistakable sounds of a violent struggle. Loud bellows. The sounds of falling furniture followed by cries of agony. Heavy, thudding sounds.

Suddenly, there was silence. Shloime knocked on the door. There was a sound of shuffling footsteps, and the door opened.

In the doorway stood a short, wizened man in a long, shabby black robe, his breath coming in labored gasps. He peered out suspiciously at his two visitors with squinting blue eyes.

"What do you want?" he demanded.

"We would like to have a word with you, sir," said Shloime. "May we come in?"

"I suppose so," Triefak said reluctantly, still gasping. "Come this way."

They followed the priest into the house. They did not ask for an explanation of the disturbance, nor did he offer any.

The floor was littered with overturned chairs. In a corner lay a torn burlap sack from which nutshells spilled all over the floor. The priest picked up two overturned chairs and placed one in front of a long, rickety table that groaned under huge piles of unwashed dishes.

"So what do you want?" he said after he had sat down. "Are

you trying to sell something? I know that I'm supposed to recognize you because you didn't tell me your names. You'll have to forgive me, though. I don't see very well. I'm afraid I don't recognize you."

"Actually, you don't know us," replied Shloime. "We didn't tell you our names because you didn't ask us. Let us introduce ourselves. My name is —"

"Wait a minute!" the priest cried, holding up his hand.

He strained forward and cocked his ear.

"There! Do you hear it?" he asked.

"No, I hear nothing."

"Listen closely."

Shloime strained to hear.

"Do you hear it now?" asked Triefak.

"All I hear is the sound of a fly buzzing."

"That's right!" exclaimed Triefak. "Watch! He's going to come out of hiding now."

A large fly emerged from behind the mantelpiece and began to fly about the room. The priest's face turned livid with rage. He ran to the door and pulled down a heavy knobbed cane that was hanging on a hook.

Bellowing loudly and brandishing the cane above his head, he began to chase the fly about the room. He crashed into chairs and sent them sprawling. The cane thudded against the walls and the ceiling repeatedly, but the fly always escaped in time.

Shloime and Elisha watched in amazement. They didn't know whether to leave or to laugh.

Finally, Elisha ran to the door, opened it wide and, flapping his hat, chased the fly into the street. Then he quickly shut the door.

"I am eternally grateful to you, sirs," gasped the priest as he collapsed into his chair. "What can I do for you?"

Shloime cleared his throat.

"Let us introduce ourselves," he said. "My name is Shloime Pulichever, and this is my associate, Elisha Ringel. We'd like to have a few words with you about the recent troubles in Pulichev."

Triefak sat bolt upright when Shloime introduced himself. He leaned forward and strained to get a better look at this famous person who had walked into his fogbound world.

How shall I handle this? he wondered. Do I speak to him as I would to an ordinary Jew or as I would to a former bishop? Agitation showed on Triefak's face as he grappled with this baffling problem.

"We want you to know," said Shloime, "that we hold you in the highest esteem. You know something of my background, don't you?"

"Oh, just a few vague things that I picked up here and there," said Triefak carefully. "I'm not very curious, and I don't like to gossip."

"Of course not. It would be beneath a man of your stature to stoop to such practices," said Shloime. "As I was saying, the years I spent in the Church have given me a special perspective on men of the cloth. I have observed your work here in Pulichev, and I think you are an exceptional shepherd for your flock. The Church is most fortunate to have a man like you."

"Thank you, sir," Triefak bubbled. "Thank you very much indeed. Sometimes I wonder if anyone appreciates how hard I work, how devoted I am to my flock. It is very encouraging to hear such kind words."

"I have to tell you though that I am quite disturbed at what has been happening in Pulichev," continued Shloime. "I'm afraid it doesn't reflect well on you."

Triefak fidgeted.

"What do you mean?" he asked suspiciously.

"Well, we've never had any trouble between gentile and Jew here in Pulichev," explained Shloime. "We've had quite a few shepherds in this parish over the years, some better, some worse, but they have all respected the traditions of harmony and peace. Until now! And I'm afraid some of the responsibility lies with you, sir."

"But what could I do?" demanded Triefak with obvious sincerity. "A messenger from Heaven directed me to do what I did. How could I refuse to do as he said?"

The priest clearly believed what he was saying. This was an unexpected development. Shloime was flustered, but he quickly recovered.

"Certainly," he said. "Did you think we were accusing you of unseemly behavior? We had no doubt that you acted honorably. We only wanted to review the situation with you."

The tension eased. Shloime reached into the inside pocket of his overcoat. He took out a bottle of slivovitz and opened it. Triefak squinted at the bottle of liquor. His eyes lit up when he recognized what it was.

"My associate here," said Shloime, pointing to Elisha, "is a man of considerable importance. He acts as an emissary for the royal houses of Europe who wish to negotiate trade agreements with the East. He has just returned from the Balkans. This bottle is part of a case that was a personal gift to him from the Turkish Sultan. We give it to you as a token of esteem."

Triefak was impressed.

"Thank you, thank you," he gushed.

He held the bottle lovingly in his hand and held it up to his nose.

"Would you gentlemen do me the honor of sharing a cup of this excellent nectar with me?" he asked.

"We would be honored," said Shloime. "In fact, we were going to suggest it ourselves. What better way is there for men to express good will towards each other than by drinking together?"

"Quite so," said Triefak.

He instinctively began to raise the bottle of liquor to his thirsty lips but stopped in midair. He coughed to cover his embarrassment.

"Excuse me a moment while I go get some drinking cups," he said.

Triefak puttered about in the kitchen and presently returned with three cups in various stages of cleanliness. He put the cups on the table and poured a healthy dollop of the liquor into his own cup and a lesser amount into those of his guests.

Shloime brought his cup to his lips without actually drinking from it.

"Excellent!" Shloime exclaimed as he returned the cup to the table. "Don't you agree, Elisha?"

"It is a liquor fit for kings and sultans," cried Elisha who had not even touched his cup. "It reminds me of the warm nights in Constantinople along the shores of the Bosporus. Why don't you have some more?"

"A toast, gentlemen! To harmony and good will!" shouted the nearsighted priest as he refilled his cup. "To peace and brotherhood among all men!"

He emptied it in one thirsty gulp and staggered for a moment as the fiery liquid surged into his bloodstream. Then he smacked his lips noisily and hiccupped.

"This liquor is really extraordinary," said Shloime. "Would you mind if we took another?"

"By all means, my honored guests, please do," he said. "And I, as a good host, shall join you."

"Splendid!" exclaimed Shloime.

Shloime filled Triefak's cup to the brim and pretended to pour some more into his own and Elisha's. Triefak immediately emptied his cup. He smiled expansively and opened his collar. The fog in which he ordinarily lived became even hazier. He could not see that Shloime and Elisha were watching him intently.

"My good friend Elisha and I were discussing you on our way here," said Shloime. "We were remarking that you must be a very special person."

"Were you really?" slurred Triefak.

"Indeed, we were," said Shloime. "Not every ordinary clergy-man receives messages from Heaven, you know. You must be an extraordinary person."

"Well, let me tell you, gentlemen, it was an unsettling exper-ience," confided Triefak, looking around him as he spoke. "I am not accustomed to receiving messages from Heaven every day, you know."

"We didn't know that," said Elisha.

"Well, it is a fact," said Triefak. "This was the first time I was visited by a messenger from Heaven. It almost scared me out of my wits."

Everything was going much better than planned. They had expected him to be hostile. They had hoped to loosen his tongue a little with the liquor. If he could be gotten to talk, they had reasoned, he might let slip some scrap of useful information. They had certainly not expected to find a muddleheaded, half-blind little man who clearly believed he had received a message from Heaven. Fortunately, they had been able to take advantage of his nearsightedness to get him intoxicated and remain totally sober themselves. They would have to tread very carefully now.

"We can well appreciate that," said Shloime. "It would frighten any man."

"I once had a similar experience in Egypt," said Elisha, winking mischievously at Shloime. "There was this fellow with a silver turban who used to conjure up spirits for us if we paid him a few small coins. His spirits didn't speak, but they did moan and groan. They looked like pieces of mist. You could see right through them."

"I don't know about those kind of spirits," said Triefak. "Maybe that's the kind they have in heathen countries like Egypt. Mine was real, I tell you. He wasn't one of your misty spirits. He stood in this room and spoke to me, just as sure as the two of you are speaking to me now."

"Did this messenger look like an ordinary human being?" asked Shloime.

"In a manner of speaking, I suppose," said Triefak. "He wore a large black cloak and a black hood that covered him completely. I could only see the glint of his eyes from inside the shadows of his hood."

Shloime turned white and inhaled sharply. The painful images of the nightmare he had had in Wielkowicz flashed through his mind.

This "messenger" was the dreadful black shadow of his

dream! He was behind the incidents that were beginning to plague the Jews of Pulichev. What other evil schemes did he have in store for them? And in the dream he had started his attack against the Rebbetzin. Could this "messenger" have something to do with his mother's illness?

"What did he say to you?" asked Shloime.

"He told me that he was the bearer of a message from Heaven to my flock," said Triefak. "As their shepherd I was chosen to deliver the message. He told me that the Jews were responsible for burning down the barn. There was no question about it. He had witnessed it himself. All I had to do was to tell my people what I had been told by the messenger from Heaven."

"What else did he say?"

"He told me that the Jews were preparing to commit a dreadful crime against the people of Pulichev," said Triefak, lowering his voice. "He told me to be alert and to be prepared to act quickly when it happened."

"Did he say what it was?"

"He said I would find out in good time."

"Tell me, did he give you a sign?" asked Shloime. "Any kind of a sign?"

"A sign?"

"I mean, how did you know he was really a messenger from Heaven?" asked Shloime. "Maybe he was just an ordinary person wrapped in a black cloak posing as a messenger from Heaven. Maybe it wasn't true."

"Oh, he was a messenger," insisted Triefak. "I'm absolutely sure of it."

"How can you be sure?"

Triefak looked at Shloime through bleary eyes. He seemed uneasy, befuddled by the liquor.

"Did he perform a miracle for you?" prompted Shloime. "You can tell us."

"I'm not supposed to tell," said Triefak reluctantly. "I shouldn't even have told you what I already did."

"Oh, you can trust us, you know," Shloime assured him. "We

won't tell him that you told us."

"Well, I guess it wouldn't matter," said Triefak doubtfully. "He told me who he was, and I know for a fact that this person is no longer alive."

"Do I know this person?" asked Shloime.

"Of course," said Triefak. "The messenger from Heaven was Zbigniew Mzlateslavski."

Zbigniew Mzlateslavski, the old priest! The "messenger" was their old enemy! Mzlateslavski had been the priest in Pulichev before Karol Triefak. He had been responsible for Shloime's abduction as a little child. He had been the one who had engineered the malicious scheme against the Jews of Krakow three years before. But Shloime and Reb Mendel had foiled his plans. His defeat had been total. His life had collapsed in ruins. Was it possible that old Mzlateslavski was the one behind all this? It couldn't be!

"You have to enlighten me," said Shloime. "I've been away for a while. I hadn't heard that he had died."

"Oh, yes, it must be about two years now," said Triefak. "Mzlateslavski was quite deranged, you know. His disastrous failure in the Krakow affair unhinged his mind. They had to keep him locked up in the old rectory in Konstantin. Such a refined man reduced to lunacy! It was pitiful, I tell you. A terrible tragedy. Well, one night he just set fire to the place and brought it crashing down on his head. The monks said they never heard such terrible screams in all their lives. He must have died an awful and painful death."

"Did they bury him?" asked Shloime.

"Bury him? You must be jesting," said Triefak. "He buried himself! There was no point in digging him out of there just to bury him all over again. They performed the funeral rites near that smoldering pile of rubble and left it there. It was a rotting old place anyway."

"Well, apparently there seems to be no doubt that he died," said Shloime. "But how do you know that he was the messenger? After all, you told us the messenger was completely covered by the cloak and the hood. Besides, your eyesight is unfortunately not the sharpest. Maybe it was someone else who was pretending to be Zbigniew Mzlateslavski. How can you be so sure it was Mzlateslavski himself?"

"Oh, there is no question that it was Father Zbigniew," said Triefak.

"But how can you be sure?"

"Oh, there's absolutely no doubt about it," insisted Triefak. "I recognized his voice."

The Darkest Hour · 7

THE REALIZATION SLOWLY SANK into Shloime's mind. Karol Triefak's recognition of Zbigniew Mzlateslavski's voice was positive proof. Apparently, the old priest had returned to haunt the Jews of Pulichev. Only, he was no messenger from Heaven. He had somehow managed to escape the burning inferno that the old rectory in Konstantin had become. Even if it had indeed been his screams that the monks had heard that night it only meant that he had been injured. His body had never been found, and there was no proof that he had died.

At last, the black shadow of Shloime's dream had assumed an identity. No longer was it a nameless phantom; it had become real.

Shloime vividly recalled the maniacal rage in Mzlateslavski's eyes, on that fateful day in Krakow, when he had realized how thoroughly Reb Mendel and Shloime had defeated and disgraced him.

So this was why the shadowy black figure in his dream had attacked his mother first! It stood to reason that Mzlateslavski would try to avenge himself on Reb Mendel and Shloime first. What more cunning and vicious way could there be than by attacking the Rebbetzin first!? What evil satisfaction Mzlateslavski must be getting from the mental anguish he was inflicting on them!

Walking back from Triefak's house, Shloime and Elisha reviewed all the facts as they knew them. They examined them from every angle, but no solution presented itself. Shloime was now convinced that Mzlateslavski was responsible for his moth-

70

er's steady deterioration. But how had he done it? Was there a cure for this mysterious illness? There was no time to waste. Something had to be done right away if his mother was to be saved. But what? Panic clutched at his throat.

When they returned, Reb Mendel was just leaving the house on his way to *shul* to prepare for the regular *shiur* he said between *Minchah* and *Maariv*. Shloime and Elisha walked along with him and told him of their horrifying discovery.

Reb Mendel was shocked to find out that his old enemy Zbigniew Mzlateslavski was hiding in Pulichev and plotting against its Jews. He had not been fully convinced of the extreme gravity of the situation, but now a cold fear gripped his heart. The danger had suddenly become so real that he could almost reach out and touch it. Yet, he had to admit, he was as baffled as they were.

Reb Mendel fell silent as they turned into the street that led to the *shul*. His steps had become slow and heavy, as if an unbearable burden had just fallen on his shoulders. Shloime and Elisha, walking on either side of him, did not disturb the silence.

Reb Mendel let out a long sigh as they stopped in front of the *shul*. For several long minutes, he stood there staring at his beloved *shul*, his second home for over forty years. Then he turned his eyes heavenward with a look of pleading more eloquent than words could possibly be.

The tension and anguish that had contorted his body seemed to melt away.

"Shloimele, we must not let ourselves become victims of despair," he finally said. "A person who trusts in the *Ribono Shel Olam* has no right to despair. In our situation we are especially fortunate because the *Ribono Shel Olam* has sent us a warning through your dream. After we finish *davening*, Elisha, you and I will sit down in my study and discuss this calmly. Perhaps we will ask Ephraim to join us, too."

Ordinarily, Reb Mendel *davened* before the *amud* only on *Shabbos* or *Yom Tov*. This day, however, he *davened Minchah* before the *amud*.

He wrapped himself in his *Shabbos tallis*, and with tears streaming from his eyes and his *tallis*-draped arms outstretched before him, he recited the *Shemoneh Esray* with passionate devotion. The very walls of the hushed chamber trembled with the tremors of Reb Mendel's body as he cried out the holy words of *Kedushah*. All who were there felt as if strength and encouragement were flowing down to them from the heavens through the conduits of those two outstretched arms.

After *Maariv*, they all gathered in the study.

"Well, *Rabbosai*," Reb Mendel said as he looked at their anxious faces. "We know now that old Zbigniew Mzlateslavski is behind the recent troubles in Pulichev. I fear that what we have seen till now is only a small taste of what the old rascal has in store for us. As I see it, we must set two objectives for ourselves. These objectives are related, but we have to approach them individually. One, we must try to find out where he is hiding and have him removed from Pulichev. Two, until we find him, we have to try and anticipate his next move and block it."

"Do you think we could have him removed if we found him?" asked Elisha.

"I'm sure that would be no problem," replied Reb Mendel. "Don't forget that the man is an escaped lunatic. As long as they believe he has died and returned as a messenger from Heaven they'll listen to him. But if he turns out to be alive they'll just lock him up again and pay no more attention to him. Ephraim, what do you say?"

"Oh, I'm sure you're right. A living Mzlateslavski on the loose is an embarrassment for the Church."

"Exactly," said Reb Mendel. "Shloimele, I think we'll begin with your dream. Let's see if we can find a clue there. Tell it to us once again in as much detail as you possibly can. Don't leave out anything, no matter how insignificant it seems."

Shloime cleared his throat and concentrated as hard as he could. Everyone in the room had already heard the dream once before; now they would be able to examine it more closely. Shloime began with the arrival of the letter that had aroused his suspicions that something was amiss. He left out no detail, not even when he was telling about how Reb Yomtov had tried to prevent his departure from Wielkowicz.

"The key, of course, is in the warning of the creature in the forest," said Reb Mendel when Shloime had finished. "Beware of the short one, were those its exact words?"

"Those were its words," said Shloime. "The creature said them twice, both times exactly the same. Beware of the short one."

"Well, who can the short one be?" asked Reb Mendel. "It cannot mean Mzlateslavski because Mzlateslavski is quite a tall man. Who else can it mean?"

"Well, Karol Triefak is a short man," suggested Elisha. "Perhaps he is the one to whom the creature was referring."

"It is possible," said Reb Mendel. "He is certainly causing a great deal of mischief."

"Perhaps it is Roman Szczyrk," suggested Ephraim. "He is a stocky fellow, but he is quite short."

"Yes, that is also a possibility," said Reb Mendel. "There is only one thing. The creature was addressing Shloime's concern about his mother. What connection can there possibly be between Triefak or Szczyrk and the Rebbetzin's illness?"

This puzzling question was met with a pensive silence for several long minutes.

"I suggest we leave the question of the short one for a while," said Reb Mendel. "Let us instead examine the dream itself. Perhaps we can find some hint in the last part of the dream. Is everyone in agreement?"

They all nodded.

"Very well," said Reb Mendel. "The most obvious point is that this giant, black-cloaked figure represented great menace for Pulichev and that the menace was first directed towards the Rebbetzin. The startling thing is that the source of the menace, Mzlateslavski, goes about wrapped in a black cloak, and indeed, the Rebbetzin has fallen mysteriously ill. This lends great credibility to the dream. Now what else can we deduce from the dream?"

"But wouldn't it seem from the dream that the menace was directed only at the Rebbetzin?" asked Ephraim Surkis. "The figure passed many other people on the main street but ignored them all."

"There is a simple explanation for that, Ephraim," said Elisha. "It probably would have turned its attention to the other people afterwards, if Reb Yomtov hadn't awakened Shloime."

"I'm sure you're right, Elisha," said Reb Mendel. "Also, if you remember, although the people didn't see it, they felt its evil presence and stepped aside. Clearly, they felt threatened by it. The reason its first target was the Rebbetzin becomes clear now that we have discovered that the creature represents Mzlateslavski. It is the kind of thing Mzlateslavski would do, especially a deranged Mzlateslavski. He would avenge himself on Shloime and myself by hurting the Rebbetzin."

"I see," said Ephraim. "I think this touches on one of the most puzzling aspects of the dream. Here is this creature that hates Reb Mendel, the Rebbetzin, Shloime and all the Jews of Pulichev. Yet, only Shloime can see it. The people of Pulichev can only *feel* its presence, while you, Reb Mendel, and the Rebbetzin are completely oblivious to it. What does this mean?"

"I don't think you can attach much significance to the fact that I can see it," said Shloime. "After all, I was the one who was having the dream."

"Quite so," said Reb Mendel, nodding his head. "But let's not discount it completely either. Maybe for some reason you, Shloimele, are in a better position to see the truth than the rest of us."

"I think there is another significant point in the dream," said Shloime. "Why does the shadowy figure wrap itself in its black cloak?"

"Well, what did you expect?" asked Elisha with a wry smile. "To see its face too?"

"Of course not, Elisha," said Shloime. "But it turns out that the person it represents, Mzlateslavski, also appears that way. Triefak never caught a glimpse of his face. He only recognized him by the sound of his voice. Why didn't he show his face? He wasn't trying to hide his identity. On the contrary, he *wanted* Triefak to know who he was. That was his proof that he was a messenger from Heaven, if you remember what Triefak told us. Wouldn't it have made sense for him to show his face?"

"That is an excellent point, Shloimele," said Reb Mendel. "We'll have to give some thought to that. Is there anything else to be deduced from the dream?"

"The business with Shloime being locked in the ring of laughing churchmen puzzles me," said Elisha. "I realize that the danger is being directed through the Church, but why are they laughing at us?"

"Yes! That is another significant point."

"I thought of an explanation of sorts," said Elisha. "I think they are laughing because we will be fighting against something foolish and ridiculous. They'll know it and we'll know it, but it won't do us any good."

"What do you mean?" asked Reb Mendel.

"It's just an impression I have, a feeling," said Elisha with a shrug of his shoulders. "I can't put my finger on it."

"Well, we'll all keep it in mind."

"I just remembered one more thing," said Shloime. "It's not part of the dream. It's some advice Reb Yomtov gave me before I left. He told me never to forget that things are not always as they seem."

Reb Mendel smiled.

"Reb Yomtov, living in little, out-of-the-way Wielkowicz, is very aware of what goes on in the world," he said. "His advice is always sound. We would do well to keep it in mind. Now, let us examine the situation here in Pulichev and see if there is anything we can do. Ephraim?"

"We know that Mzlateslavski is in contact with Triefak," said Ephraim. "I suspect that he has also been in contact with Roman Szczyrk."

"What makes you say that?" asked Reb Mendel in a puzzled voice. "I didn't hear anything to indicate any connection between Mzlateslavski and Szczyrk."

"Well, for one thing, he was the leader of the peasants that burned down the barns of the Jews," replied Ephraim. "But even more, I don't think it would be enough for Mzlateslavski to contact Triefak only. True, Triefak can be used to stir up the gentiles of Pulichev, but Mzlateslavski would still need someone to carry out his specific instructions. Who would be a more likely candidate than a troublemaker like Szczyrk? I'm sure Szczyrk would do anything that Mzlateslavski wanted as long as he was offered a reward."

"But what kind of reward could Mzlateslavski offer him now that he is in hiding?" asked Shloime.

"That really doesn't make a difference to us at this point," said Reb Mendel. "But knowing Mzlateslavski, you can be sure he'll come up with something."

"So, why don't we have Triefak and Szczyrk watched?" suggested Elisha. "Then, if Mzlateslavski makes contact with them again we can follow him and discover his hiding place."

"I think Elisha is right," said Shloime. "This should be our first step."

"But it can also backfire," cautioned Reb Mendel. "We must be exceedingly careful."

"What do you mean, Father?" asked Shloime. "How can it backfire on us?"

"Because if it becomes known that we are watching them there is bound to be a lot of resentment towards us," explained Reb Mendel. "Whatever we do we must be very discreet. We don't want to cause any new problems for ourselves."

"If only Kalman Kalb could talk," said Ephraim wistfully, "he would be the perfect choice to keep an eye on Triefak and Szczyrk. He is always roaming the streets at night. No one pays him any attention."

"Come to think of it," said Elisha, "if Kalman Kalb could talk there is probably a lot of valuable information he could tell us right now."

"What do you mean?" asked Reb Mendel sharply.

"Like Ephraim says, he is always roaming about in the evenings," said Elisha. "I'm sure he's already seen some things that would help us if we knew about them. I wouldn't be surprised if he has seen Mzlateslavski. Maybe he even knows where Mzlateslavski is hiding."

"I agree with Ephraim and Elisha," said Shloime. "Father, you and Mother know Kalman Kalb better than anyone. He trusts you. Do you think there is any possible way to get him to tell us what he knows?"

"I wish there were," said Reb Mendel, "but he's been here almost two years and—"

A loud hammering on the front door cut Reb Mendel off in midsentence. Shloime and Ephraim both ran to the door to see who it was. It was a Jewish tradesman who lived on the next street. His face was a flaming red, and he was out of breath. Between gasps, he asked to see Reb Mendel. Ephraim showed him into the study, while Shloime ran to bring him a glass of water.

"Rebbe!" he cried out as soon as he saw Reb Mendel. "There is a terrible rumor going around Pulichev. They are saying that a Christian child has disappeared. They are saying that the Jews are responsible, that we need the blood of a Christian for the preparation of the *matzos* for *Pesach*, that we've killed the child and drained its blood."

Reb Mendel recoiled in shock.

"A blood libel!" he cried out, grabbing his head with both hands. "Heaven protect us!"

His message delivered, the flustered tradesman took the glass of water from Shloime's hand. He gulped the water down and left. The others remained frozen in their places, staring at each other in disbelief.

Could it be that there would be a blood libel in Pulichev? Was this the diabolical scheme that Mzlateslavski had devised to destroy the Jews of Pulichev?

Blood libel!

The very words struck terror in the hearts of Jews all over Europe. Ever since the first blood libel had first been fabricated hundreds of years before, it had been used repeatedly against Jewish communities all across Europe, from England to Russia. Almost always it had resulted in pogroms and slaughter. The perpetrators of this libel claimed that the Jews had a mysterious ritual for baking their *matzos* that required the addition of fresh human blood, preferably the blood of a Christian. Sometimes, they would produce a body that had allegedly been used. Sometimes, they wouldn't even bother to do that, relying only on an unexplained disappearance of a Christian child to support their claim.

The Church itself had come out against blood libels. Cardinals and bishops had issued proclamations stating that there was absolutely no basis for these accusations. But the blood libels persisted. And innocent Jewish blood was spilled to avenge these groundless and ridiculous charges. Once the gentile populace had been whipped into a frenzy there was no stopping them.

Reb Mendel looked about at the terrified faces.

"Rabbosai!" he cried out. "Are we to be reduced to helpless children by the sound of these words? Are we to be so easily defeated? What has happened to our *bitachon?* Has it just evaporated like the morning mist? The Jews of Pulichev need us. We must not lose ourselves."

"What would you have us do, Father?" asked Shloime, his voice barely audible, his face ashen.

"First we have to calm down. We have to try and anticipate Mzlateslavski's next move. There has always been peace between the Jews and gentiles of Pulichev. A blood libel will not be successful with just a disappearance. I think we can be sure that the child's dead body will be discovered, drained of its blood. And I wouldn't be surprised if Roman Szczyrk will be the one to discover it."

Reb Mendel paused, his brows furrowed with concentration. The others waited silently for him to continue.

"I'm also reasonably sure that even the discovery of a dead Christian child will not be enough for a blood libel to be successful in Pulichev," he continued as he pulled worriedly at his beard.

"Oh, it's one thing to go out and burn some barns simply because a misguided priest claims he received a message from Heaven. But it's quite another thing to start a pogrom on such a basis. They will want to be convinced that the Jews are indeed responsible, that it is not a plot."

"Are you sure of this?" asked Elisha.

"No. Unfortunately, I am not sure of this," he replied. "But I have lived in Pulichev most of my life. And this is what I think."

"Are you then saying that we have nothing to fear?" asked Ephraim. "Are you saying that all Mzlateslavski's efforts will be for naught?"

"I'm afraid not, my dear Ephraim," said Reb Mendel. "I'm afraid not. If I know this then you can be sure that Mzlateslavski knows this as well. Don't forget, Pulichev was his parish for many years. He won't be satisfied with an unsubstantiated accusation, even a body. I think that he will try to produce something more substantial."

"Like what?" asked Ephraim.

"Perhaps a witness," suggested Elisha. "Someone who will claim he saw the Jews abducting a Christian child."

"I don't think so," said Shloime. "Whom could he get? Roman Szczyrk? The people wouldn't believe him. He would have to risk making contact with someone else. And it would have to be someone dishonest enough to lie for him yet reputable enough to convince the people. I don't think this will be his approach."

"So what do we do?" asked Ephraim.

"I think we should all try to get some rest," said Reb Mendel. "Tomorrow promises to be a difficult day."

"You think something might happen during the night?" asked Ephraim.

"It is a possibility."

"Then perhaps I should sleep here tonight," said Ephraim. "I'll just run home and tell Bracha. I'll return shortly."

"Fine," said Reb Mendel. "Let us pray that the *Ribono Shel Olam* will give us the courage and the wisdom to save the Jews of

Pulichev from this evil scheme. Go to sleep, my children. We must rise early tomorrow."

Ephraim put on his coat and left, and Shloime and Elisha went upstairs. When Ephraim returned he found Reb Mendel bent over his *Tehillim*. Ephraim did not disturb him. He went up the stairs soundlessly and went straight to sleep.

It was still very dark when they were awakened by a commotion in the street. Reb Mendel was the first to hear it and rushed to rouse the others.

Shloime and Ephraim were awake in an instant, but Elisha was nowhere to be found. He had not been seen since the previous evening when he had supposedly gone up to sleep. No one knew where he had gone. But there was no time to go looking for him. Ephraim set off to find out the cause of the commotion and to check on his family. Reb Mendel and Shloime went to make sure that the house was securely locked.

The darkness was beginning to fade when Ephraim returned, bringing his wife and children with him. He had found a heavy club and would not let it out of his grasp.

Reb Mendel had been right, he reported. During the night, Roman Szczyrk had "found" the body of the missing Christian child. It had been completely drained of blood. Szczyrk had run around the gentile sections of Pulichev shouting at the top of his lungs and waking the entire populace.

Word was spreading like wildfire. The entire city was awake and in an uproar. Word had even reached the peasants in the outlying areas, and they were streaming towards the city.

Pandemonium greeted Reb Mendel, Shloime and Ephraim as they stepped into the street. Panic and confusion gripped the Jewish section of Pulichev. Many families were busy barricading their houses against the anticipated pogrom. Others had hastily hitched up horses to their wagons and were bundling a pitiful few belongings into them as they prepared to flee. Here and there, a mother crooned to a small child crying from fright that it felt but did not understand. Or a father spoke solemnly to his young son about dying *al Kiddush Hashem*. Most of the people just milled about the streets, numb with desperation.

The final blow fell just as the day was breaking. It was reported that a huge mob was heading towards the Jewish section. Their destination was the main *shul*. Somehow the rumor had spread among the enraged gentile populace that a flask containing the blood of the murdered child was hidden in the *shul*. The mob was prepared to tear the *shul* apart to find the flask. If they found it they would have all the "evidence" they needed.

As soon as he heard this report Reb Mendel started to run towards the *shul* as quickly as his aged legs would carry him. Shloime and Ephraim immediately set off after him.

When they arrived at the *shul* the street was still empty, but they could hear the rumble of the approaching mob. Reb Mendel planted himself directly in front of the door. He stood facing the oncoming, though as yet unseen, mob. Shloime and Ephraim positioned themselves on either side of him.

"My children," Reb Mendel said, his voice strangely calm. "Even now, as the sound of the approaching mob grows more deafening by the moment, we must not despair. We must never lose *bitachon* in the *Ribono Shel Olam*. And if we are meant to die we must give ourselves up gladly *al Kiddush Hashem.*"

He paused for a moment then continued.

"I hope Elisha is all right," he said. "I am concerned for his safety. Where could he have gone in middle of the night? Didn't he say anything at all last night, Shloime?"

"No, Father, he didn't."

"And I'm also concerned for your mother," said Reb Mendel, seemingly oblivious to the great peril he himself was facing. "She has probably been awakened by all the noise. She will be frightened."

"You needn't worry about the Rebbetzin," said Ephraim. "Bracha will take care of her. She will be fine."

"Of course, Ephraim," said Reb Mendel. "Thank you for your reassurance. Your Bracha is a very good person. May the *Ribono Shel Olam* protect her and your wonderful children."

At that moment, the mob surged into sight. Roman Szczyrk was in the front, screaming and brandishing a blacksmith's hammer. Others were carrying all sorts of other weapons and waving them about. Many of them were carrying rocks in their hands, as if they had grabbed the first thing that came to hand. The combined sound of their frenzied shouts was like an avalanche. It grew louder and louder and louder still.

At the last moment, Reb Mendel stepped forward and lifted his arms, his open palms facing the approaching mob. The startled mob came to a halt less than ten paces from Reb Mendel and his companions, but its anger and hatred reached out like a huge blanket to engulf them. Roman Szczyrk stepped forward.

"Get out of the way, Jew," shouted the blacksmith. "We want to see where you have hidden the blood of the poor Christian child you murdered. Step aside or we will trample you."

"We have not murdered any Christian child," shouted Reb Mendel. "The Jewish people abhor blood. There is no blood to be found in our synagogue."

"Step aside and we will look for ourselves," commanded the blacksmith. "We will see for ourselves if you are telling the truth or if you are lying to cover your guilt."

"Tell your friends to go away," said Reb Mendel, "and I myself will take you in and let you search to your heart's content. That should surely be enough. There is no need for a mob entering this hallowed place."

Suddenly, there was a thud against the wall of the *shul*. Someone in the center of the mob had hurled a rock. It had missed its target, but the spell was broken. A barrage of rocks rained down on the three trapped Jews, and the mob surged forward.

Shloime pushed Reb Mendel to the ground and fell upon him, using his own body to shield his father. Ephraim stood at their side and began to swing his club wildly in a desperate attempt to drive off the mob, until he finally collapsed, his life-blood draining out of his wounds. Shloime and Reb Mendel braced themselves for the end.

At that moment, another sound joined the roar of the mob. The thundering of horses' hooves froze the mob, then threw it into confusion. A group of twenty horsemen came galloping down the street.

The horsemen rode straight at the mob, which split before the flying hooves, and stopped in front of the *shul*. Most of the horsemen were the soldiers of the count, except for two of them. One of these was Karol Triefak. The other was Elisha Ringel.

The Deadline · 8

E LISHA RINGEL HAD BEEN UNABLE to sleep the night before; his sense of imminent danger was too strong. After the others had fallen asleep, he took whatever money he had and slipped out of the house. He awakened the Jewish owner of a nearby stable and hired a swift horse. Then riding as fast as an untrained horseman could, he set off for Malonavka.

It took him two hours to get there. Although it was almost midnight, he went straight to the residence of Jan Bilutsa, the Bishop of Malonavka, and pounded on the door. The servants tried to chase away this wild-eyed young Jew, but he screamed that he had an urgent message for the bishop, that if they didn't let it through they would be held responsible. Unwilling to risk the bishop's displeasure, they showed him in.

Jan Bilutsa was annoyed at this midnight intrusion. But when Elisha reminded him of that afternoon in the old city of Krakow when he had offered to come to Shloime's assistance if he should ever need it, Bilutsa reluctantly agreed to hear him out. Speaking rapidly, Elisha told him about what was happening in Pulichev. His words came tumbling out in an agitated torrent of fact, impression and speculation.

Bilutsa grew increasingly concerned as he listened to Elisha's account. It seemed that the deranged old priest Zbigniew Mzlateslavski had not perished in the burning rectory, as had been assumed. Apparently, he had returned to Pulichev and was planning a blood libel against its Jews. The disappearance of the Christian child indicated that Mzlateslavski was ready to make his final move.

There would be repercussions if he were successful, thought Bilutsa. The count would suffer heavy financial losses and would be furious. The church would suffer embarrassment; the cardinal and maybe even the pope would be annoyed. And since Pulichev was in Bilutsa's diocese, he would have to answer to his superiors for anything that happened there. Things could become quite unpleasant, thought Bilutsa.

The obvious course was to send a message to Pulichev stating that the accusations were completely groundless and ordering that they be ignored. But unfortunately, it was not so simple. Once the populace, especially the ignorant peasantry, had been inflamed by a blood libel, a simple order to ignore the accusations would be totally inadequate.

The problem facing Bilutsa was a very delicate one. On the one hand, he had to prevent the bloodbath that threatened the Jews of Pulichev. On the other hand, he had to devise a plan that would not enrage the bloodthirsty, frenzied mob. And he had very little time in which to do it.

Bilutsa considered the problem calmly and carefully. He sat absolutely still for a long time and examined the problem again and again. Elisha fidgeted nervously as he watched the motionless bishop, trying hard to discern the thoughts passing through his head.

Finally, Bilutsa decided on a course of action. He wrote two notes and affixed them with his personal seal. One was addressed to Count Leszek Bernowiecz apprising him of the situation and requesting that he send a detachment of soldiers to Pulichev immediately. The second was addressed to Karol Triefak. It commanded him to suspend action on any blood accusation until he, Bilutsa, would arrive in Pulichev. He would be arriving in three days, at which time he would conduct an official and thorough investigation. Any impatient person who took any action before the results of the investigation were released would be excommunicated from the church. It was Triefak's responsibility to maintain order among the populace of Pulichev until Bilutsa arrived.

The bishop gave the two notes to Elisha and told him to deliver them immediately.

Ignoring the numbing exhaustion that gripped his body, Elisha rode back towards Pulichev at reckless speed, stopping only at Bernowiecz Castle along the way.

After carefully inspecting the bedraggled midnight rider, the guards lowered the drawbridge across the moat and went to awaken the count. The count looked closely at the bishop's seal. Then he had read the note with a growing expression of gravity on his face. He read it through once again and then summoned the captain of the guard, a burly man named Pyotr Tambok. He assigned a detachment of the most seasoned cavalrymen among the castle guard to Tambok and dispatched them immediately to Pulichev.

The darkness was already beginning to fade when Elisha, accompanied by the count's troops, stopped at Karol Triefak's house. Triefak was already awake when they arrived. The stunning news of the discovery of the missing child's body had already reached him. He was pacing about and muttering to himself, unsure of how to react. The rapid pace of events had overwhelmed the little priest.

Elisha delivered the bishop's note to the flustered priest. Triefak read the note with growing alarm. He told Elisha and the soldiers what was going on in Pulichev. The soldiers hoisted Triefak onto one of the spare horses and they had all set off for the *shul* at a full gallop.

As they entered the Jewish section of Pulichev, morning had already broken. The angry roar of the mob assaulted them as a blast of hot air from the door of a furnace. As they turned into the street that led to the *shul* Elisha was sickened by the ugly scene that unfolded before him. The *shul* was completely surrounded by the swarming mob. Rocks flew through the air. The terror in Elisha's heart gave way to despair.

A hoarse cry escaped from his throat as he spurred his horse to even greater speed. The horse responded with a burst of speed, and the other horses strained to keep pace. He pointed his horse straight at the center of the mob.

The mob melted away before the charging horses, and the riders came to a stop directly in front of the *shul*.

Reb Mendel lay on the ground with Shloime sprawled on top of him. Beside them lay the lifeless body of Ephraim Surkis, his face covered with gashes and bruises, the club still clutched tightly in his fists.

The soldiers wheeled into a semicircle protecting the entrance to the *shul*. Karol Triefak stood up high in the saddle and addressed the mob.

The Bishop of Malonavka has sent instructions, he shouted, and a detachment of cavalry to enforce them. You are all to return to your homes. I am delegated to collect the evidence and present it to the bishop when he arrives three days hence. Fear not, he shouted, the truth shall not be concealed.

The mob could have easily overrun the cavalrymen, and a half hour earlier it might indeed have been inclined to do so. But its manic momentum had been interrupted, and the arrival of the horsemen and the bishop's message had further disrupted it. The intensity fizzled and died. Suddenly, this monstrous, surging, unified mass of humanity was once again reduced to its simple elements. It became merely a shuffling crowd of confused people. Grumbling and shaking their heads, the crowd slowly dispersed.

Reb Mendel remained sitting on the ground next to Ephraim's dead body, weeping bitterly and rocking back and forth. Shloime and Elisha stood beside him in griefstricken silence. Karol Triefak and the cavalrymen of the castle guard stayed a short distance away.

Finally, Pyotr Tambok, the captain of the guard, dismounted and approached. He took off his cap as a gesture of respect and cleared his throat.

"Gentlemen, you have my heartfelt sympathy," he began. "Your friend must have been a very valiant young man."

There was no response. Only weeping. And silence.

"Gentlemen, I don't want to intrude on your bereavement,"

continued Captain Tambok, "but I have a mission to fulfill. I have been instructed by my lord, Count Leszek Bernowiecz, to gather whatever evidence there may be. Jan Bilutsa, the Bishop of Malo-navka, will be arriving in three days time and will conduct an investigation."

Some other Jewish men had arrived on the scene and were gathering around Reb Mendel. Reb Mendel stood up and turned to face Tambok.

"It has been alleged that there is a flask of blood concealed in your synagogue," continued Tambok, not without embarrass-ment. "It has been alleged that it contains the blood of a mur-dered Christian child. I have no choice in the matter. My men and I will have to search the synagogue. Will you unlock the door for us? You may join us if you wish."

Reb Mendel nodded slowly. Leaving Ephraim's body in the care of the Jewish men who had just arrived, he took the key from his pocket and trudged to the front door. Tambok followed close behind. Reb Mendel put the key in the lock and turned it. He was about to open the door when he suddenly remembered something.

"Before we go in there is something I must tell you," he said to Tambok. "There is an old man who always sleeps in the *shul*. He is a simple man, a mute. His name is Kalman Kalb. I'm sure he is cowering inside, confused and afraid. If we all burst in on him together we are likely to frighten him out of his wits. Would you mind if I go in first and reassure him?"

"Of course," said Tambok. "I alone will accompany you. Have you any objections, Father Karol?"

"None at all," replied the priest.

Reb Mendel and Pyotr Tambok went into the *shul*, but Kalman Kalb was nowhere to be seen. The others quickly crowded in behind them. Shloime and Elisha moved to Reb Mendel's side. The soldiers spread out over the *shul*.

Suddenly, there was a startled cry from one of the soldiers at the rear of the *shul*.

"I've found him!" he cried out.

Kalman Kalb was lying on the floor behind the last bench, the one on which he usually slept. There was a large gash across his forehead around which the blood had started to congeal. He was unconscious, but he was breathing.

"Kalman!" Reb Mendel cried in alarm.

A soldier brought a jug of water. Reb Mendel poured some of it between Kalman Kalb's lips and used the rest to bathe his face. A soldier who had seen many battlefield wounds examined the gash on Kalman Kalb's forehead. It looked worse than it actually was, he said. The old fellow would be fine, except for a few days of severe headaches.

Kalman Kalb's eyes opened. He took one look at the soldiers and let out a piercing scream. He pulled himself loose from Reb Mendel's grip and scurried away to huddle in a corner. Shloime tried to calm him down, but Kalman Kalb wouldn't budge. He just remained sitting on the floor in a corner of the *shul*, like a cornered animal. Whenever someone tried to approach him he would start to tremble and shriek.

"The old fellow seems to be all right," said Pyotr Tambok. "Let's just leave him there and get on with the business at hand. Don't worry about him. He'll calm down after a while if everyone leaves him alone."

"Yes, I agree with the captain," said Karol Triefak. "The sooner we get this matter resolved the better."

Tambok gave the order, and the soldiers began searching the *shul*.

Tambok himself went to the front of the *shul*. He opened the deep drawer in the bottom of the *Aron Hakodesh* and took everything out. He examined each *tallis* and each pair of *tefillin* separately and returned it neatly to the drawer. He found nothing. Then he pulled aside the *paroches* and peered into the *Aron Hakodesh* itself. He started to pull out the *Sifrei Torah*, but Reb Mendel ran and grabbed his arm.

"Please, good sir," he pleaded. "These scrolls are sacred to our people. Would you let me, my son and our young friend hold the scrolls while you look inside?"

"Certainly," Tambok said sympathetically. "I'll only be a moment, then you can put them back."

Reb Mendel took out the *Sifrei Torah* and handed them to Shloime and Elisha. They each took one in their arms. They laid the rest on a table and covered them with a *tallis*. Reb Mendel kept the last *Sefer Torah* himself.

Tambok reached into the now empty, dark recesses of the *Aron Hakodesh*. He groped about for a while without finding anything. Then his body tensed. Slowly, he withdrew his hand. It held a long, narrow flask. The flask was filled with a dark fluid. There could be no question about what that fluid was. The blood of the murdered Christian child had been found.

Karol Triefak's mouth fell open in shock. Reb Mendel turned deathly pale. Shloime and Elisha stared incredulously at the dark flask in Tambok's hand. Triefak was the first to break the awful silence.

"They were right! They were right!" he shouted, jumping up and down. "The Jews are guilty after all. Oh, heaven help us! We must protect our innocent Christian children from these blood-thirsty Jews."

"It is a lie!" shouted Reb Mendel in pain and rage. "I swear by the holy *Sefer Torah* that I am holding in my arms that we are completely innocent."

"Then why is the flask here?" demanded Triefak.

"Someone put it here," said Shloime.

"Who?"

"The person who engineered this entire plot," said Shloime. "This whole thing is obviously a plot against the Jewish people of Pulichev."

"How did this person get in?" demanded Triefak. "Does he have a key to the synagogue?"

Shloime was at a loss for a reply.

"Aha!" exclaimed Triefak triumphantly. "He doesn't answer because there *is* no answer. If a Christian had hidden the blood in the synagogue he would have had to come in before it was locked up. Someone definitely would have seen him. No, there can be no doubt about it. The Jews are responsible."

"Wait a minute!" exclaimed Shloime. "Kalman Kalb often goes out in the evenings when the streets are empty. He leaves the door unlocked while he's out. Maybe someone slipped in and hid the flask while he was out."

"That is nonsense," declared Triefak, pointing an accusing finger at Shloime. "The streets were anything but empty last night. I doubt if the old fool stuck as much as a toe out of the synagogue last night."

"Well, how do you explain Kalman Kalb's being struck on the head?" asked Shloime.

"It was an accident," said Triefak with a careless shrug. "He fell."

"A coincidence?"

"Then how do *you* explain it?" countered Triefak.

"I say that the person who broke into the *shul* to hide the flask was not expecting to find Kalman Kalb here," said Shloime. "Taken by surprise, he struck him a blow to the head."

"Then this person left Kalb unconscious, walked out the door and locked it behind him?" asked Triefak in a mocking voice.

"Maybe this person came and left through a window," said Shloime without conviction.

"Through a window!?" scoffed Triefak. "But the only windows I see are barred. A man couldn't fit through those."

"A small man such as yourself could."

Triefak bristled.

"Are you going to accuse me now?" he cried in outrage. "Do you think I am responsible?"

"I said nothing of the sort," replied Shloime. "I only said that someone as small as you could get through those windows."

"Maybe you are right," said Triefak, a look of sudden inspiration appearing on his face.

He pointed an accusing finger at Elisha.

"Maybe your short friend here is the real culprit," he said. "Maybe the Jews of Pulichev are actually innocent. Maybe this man, acting on his own, murdered the child and saved its blood in a flask. He wanted to hide it in the synagogue, but he didn't want anyone to see him. So he squeezed in between the bars in the middle of the night and hid the flask."

"That is preposterous!" shouted Shloime. He glared at Triefak.

"How do you know that it's not true? You told me yourself that your friend travels in the East. He even admitted that he went to people who conjure up spirits. How do you know what strange customs he picked up in those heathen countries? What a perfect solution! It will make everyone happy."

"What utter foolishness!" shouted Shloime, tears of frustration springing to his eyes.

"Seize him! Seize the little Jew!" Triefak screamed at Tambok.

Elisha made no move.

Pyotr Tambok had been silent throughout this entire exchange.

"I won't arrest anyone now, Father Karol," said the captain of the guard. "If you have any accusations to make, Father Karol, prepare them well and present them to the bishop when he arrives. As for you, gentlemen, the evidence against your people is quite strong. Do not take it lightly. The bishop arrives in three days time. Prepare to defend yourselves."

Ephraim Surkis was laid to rest that afternoon in the Jewish cemetery behind Pulichev. All the Jews of Pulichev and hundreds more from neighboring towns gathered to honor the slain young man. His family in distant Zamosc was, of course, unable to attend. It would be several days before the shocking news even reached them. But Bracha's father, Reb Asher Sofer, lived in nearby Molodietz and was already in Pulichev by midmorning. He stopped to see the Rebbetzin, his sister, who tried to console him, even as she herself lay sobbing on her bed.

The stunned and griefstricken people walked along behind the coffin in a funeral procession that stretched as far as the eye could see. They wept bitter tears for this warm, outgoing young man who had died *al Kiddush Hashem*. They wept for his young wife and small children who were now left alone. And they wept for themselves, for the terrible sword that had cut down this young man and still remained poised over all of Pulichev and its surroundings.

At the graveside, Bracha Surkis wept softly, her children clinging tightly to her side. Reb Asher Sofer started to say the *hesped* for his young son-in-law, but he broke down and could not continue. In his stead, Reb Mendel was asked to speak.

Reb Mendel was weak from sorrow and exhaustion. He tottered to his feet, leaning heavily on Shloime for support, and began to speak. He spoke briefly, his voice hardly above a whisper, his words punctuated by wrenching sobs. Even those people too far away to hear him could clearly see his love for his young nephew and his profound sense of loss.

It was a somber group of people that streamed back into Pulichev through the lengthening shadows of the dusk. The *Shiva* period of formal mourning had begun for the immediate family of Ephraim Surkis, but in actuality, all of the Jews of Pulichev mourned his loss.

Upon returning home, Reb Mendel went up to see his wife. The Rebbetzin's condition had drastically deteriorated. Her cramps and nausea had become so severe that she had difficulty eating even the few meager spoonfuls of porridge that had been her only source of nourishment for months. The choking spasms were coming more frequently and left her gasping for air on the verge of unconsciousness. She had become horribly emaciated and had begun to experience bouts of delirium. She could not last much longer in this state.

They sat together for a long while, seeking to draw strength from each other as they had done so often in the past. They shed tears together over the tragedy that had befallen them. They spoke of happier times when the Jews of Poland had lived in relative peace and security. They spoke of how the *Ribono Shel Olam* had never forsaken them in their desperate hour of need. They spoke of their beloved son Shloime and their hopes for his future, even if they themselves would not live to see it. They even found comfort in sitting together in silence, lost in their own thoughts.

Shloime and Elisha were waiting for Reb Mendel in the study when he came down. They stood up and remained standing until he had settled in his chair.

"Father, you look very pale," said Shloime. "You should get some rest. Elisha and I have been talking while we were waiting for you. We do not have much time. The bishop arrives the day after tomorrow. We have to find the answers before then, and we have to be able to prove them to the bishop's satisfaction. It will not be enough to present a plausible explanation of the facts. The blood was found in our *shul*, and unless we can prove our innocence we will be assumed guilty. All of us."

"Do you have any ideas?" asked Reb Mendel.

"Not really," said Shloime.

Elisha simply shook his head.

"Then I suggest that the both of you also get some rest," said Reb Mendel. "Tomorrow we will all wake up with clearer minds."

"Yes, we will," said Shloime. "But first we wanted to ask you a few questions, if you are up to it."

"What do I know that you don't?" asked Reb Mendel.

"It's about Kalman Kalb," said Shloime.

Reb Mendel's eyes narrowed.

"What about Kalman Kalb?" he asked.

"Elisha and I are convinced that the answers are locked in Kalman Kalb's mind," explained Shloime. "He was in the *shul* when the intruder hid the flask of blood. He must have seen the intruder; otherwise, why was he struck that blow on the head? And also, he often roams the streets at night. It is very possible that he saw something that might be useful to us, even if he himself has no way of appreciating its importance."

"What you are saying is probably true," said Reb Mendel. "But that information might as well be at the bottom of the sea. It is beyond our reach."

"We have to try anyway," insisted Shloime. "What else can

we do? We must try."

Reb Mendel sighed.

"Well, what did you want to ask me?"

"What do you know about Kalman Kalb, Father?" asked Shloime. "From where did he come? Does he have any family?"

"As far as I know he is from Gdryna," said Reb Mendel.

"Where is that?" asked Elisha. "I've been all over Poland, and I never heard of Gdryna."

"It's a small town outside of Warsaw, Elisha," said Reb Mendel. "It is unlikely you would have come across it in your travels."

"Perhaps, but how do we know he comes from Gdryna?" asked Elisha. "He can't talk or communicate with us. How do we even know that his name is Kalman Kalb?"

Reb Mendel smiled.

"That is a very obvious question," he said. "Come to think of it, I'm surprised you didn't ask me before how we knew his name was Kalman Kalb."

"Well, I never really gave him much thought," said Elisha.

"Unfortunately, no one gives him much thought," said Reb Mendel in a sad voice.

They waited in silence for Reb Mendel to continue. Indecision played across Reb Mendel's face. Finally, he spoke.

"What I am going to tell you is known to no one other than the Rebbetzin," he said quietly. "I have never felt it necessary for anyone else to know. I expect you to keep it to yourselves. Do I have your word?"

They both nodded.

"When Kalman Kalb came to Pulichev he was in worse condition than he is now," began Reb Mendel. "He would shy away if anyone came close to him. He would sit in the back of the *shul*, far away from the other people, and take out a small *Siddur* from his knapsack. Although he never read from it, he would hold it open in his hands and stare at it intently. Sometimes it seemed to me that he was crying, but I could never be sure.

"One day, I walked over to him and asked if I could take a look at his *Siddur*. He looked at me blankly; he hadn't understood a word I had said. I pointed at the *Siddur* and gestured that I would like to look at it. He seemed to understand me then, but he didn't seem inclined to hand it over. I asked him again and again until he reluctantly handed it to me.

"The *Siddur* was quite old and worn. I looked at the flyleaf. It belonged to Kalman Kalb of Gdryna. And it told me quite a bit about the man. It told me when he was born, the names of his parents and the dates of their deaths, whom he had married, the names and ages of his children and other assorted markings that I couldn't decipher. I told the people about the name I had found on the flyleaf of the Siddur, but I did not mention what else I had found there.

"Then I wrote a letter to an old friend of mine in Warsaw, telling him only that I had found an old *Siddur*. I sent him the information from the flyleaf and asked him to make some discreet inquiries for me. About two months later I received a reply to my letter.

"Kalman Kalb had indeed lived in Gdryna with his family some years before. He was a simple man who earned his living as a mason. Then he had inherited a great deal of money from an uncle in Krakow. He had sold his home in Gdryna, packed his family and his belongings into his wagon and set off for the distant city Krakow.

"He never arrived in Krakow. Nor anywhere else. He and his family were never heard from again. There were rumors that they had been attacked by bandits, but these rumors were never confirmed. My friend in Warsaw suggested that I keep the *Siddur*, since the rightful owner was unlikely to turn up.

"Clearly, the rumors were true, only Kalman Kalb himself managed to escape, though not unharmed. The shock of his loss had robbed him of his power of speech and his sanity. By the time I received the reply to my letter Kalman Kalb had settled into a normal life of sorts here in Pulichev. Apparently, he had nowhere else to go. I saw no point in revealing what I had discovered, and I never did except to your mother. I sometimes wonder where else poor Kalman has been and how he lived before he reached

Pulichev. It is a sad story.

"That is all that I know."

Shloime rose and motioned to Elisha to follow suit.

"Thank you very much, Father," he said. "We will not disturb you any more. Good night."

"Good night. Don't stay up too late."

Shloime rose early the next morning. He slipped out of the house quietly and went to the *shul* to *daven Shacharis* with the early *minyan*. Kalman Kalb was in his usual place on the last bench, but this time, Shloime looked at him in a new light. After *Shacharis*, he moved to a corner of the *shul*, saying *Tehillim* and praying silently for the safety of Pulichev and the recovery of his mother.

As it was still quite early, Shloime decided to go for a walk before returning home. He could not get the image of Kalman Kalb out of his mind. He was convinced that if he could unlock the information in Kalman Kalb's mind it would lead him to Mzlateslavski. But how? It seemed like an impossible task.

He walked and walked, oblivious to his surroundings, totally absorbed in his thoughts. Presently, he found himself out of Pulichev walking up the gentle slope of a tree-covered hillside. He looked up at the sun and was surprised to see that it was almost noon. He had completely lost track of time.

He sat down to rest for a while on a low boulder in the shade of a tree. From this vantage point, he could see Pulichev as it spread down the slope into the valley and up to the banks of the Grizdna River. There were no people on the hillside as far as the eye could see. Dominating the Jewish section was the massive old *shul* with its white stucco walls and red roof. In the distance lay the apple orchards for which Pulichev was famous. It was a lovely, peaceful scene.

It struck Shloime that this was the scene from his dream. Looking across to the facing hillside he could almost imagine the huge black shadow detaching itself from among the trees and hovering over an unsuspecting Pulichev. Shloime shivered as the dream flashed through his mind once again in sharp, painful detail, as if he had dreamed it only yesterday.

What was the key to the dream? wondered Shloime. The mocking laughter of the churchmen could be explained by the fact that blood libels were such ridiculous but nevertheless effective accusations. The attack on his mother was explained by the discovery that the black shadow was none other than Zbigniew Mzlateslavski. But why hadn't Reb Mendel been aware of its presence at all? Why had only he, Shloime, been able to see the black shadow? Why did it never show its face?

And the biggest question of all remained. Who was "the short one"? Shloime was thoroughly baffled by this question. Even the absurd possibility that it might be Elisha Ringel crossed his mind for an instant before he dismissed it.

"Ribono Shel Olam!" he cried out, rising to his feet. "You sent me the warning through my dream, but I cannot decipher its meaning. Please, please let me understand the warning so that I can save my mother's life and avert this terrible danger that hangs over all the Jews of Pulichev."

He looked up at the heavens with intense yearning, then he slumped back down on the boulder. He hunched his shoulders forward and put his head in his hands, pleading silently with the *Ribono Shel Olam* to take pity on them. He sat that way for a while when a sudden call disturbed his concentration.

"Young man!"

Shloime looked up with a start. An old peasant woman stood before him looking at him with distinct disapproval. Shloime stared at her with amazement. From where had she appeared? Just a few minutes before, he was certain, there had been no one on the entire hillside.

"Young man," said the old woman. "You look as if all the worries of the world are on your shoulders."

Shloime looked up at the old woman. Her eyes were filled with kindness and concern.

"I feel that way too," he said with a wry smile.

"Is there anything I can do to help you?" she asked.

Shloime shook his head.

"I'm afraid not," he replied. "Thank you for your kindness."

"Heaven will help you, young man, you will see," said the old woman. "In the meantime, could you show me the road into Pulichev?"

"I will show it to you," said Shloime and stood up.

"Why, you are quite a tall young man," said the old woman with apparent amazement. "Sitting there on that low boulder with your head in your hands I thought you were a short man."

"Perhaps," said Shloime impatiently. "Now, look over there, between those trees. Do you see the ones to which I'm pointing? Well, right between those trees you can see the road. Just follow that road. It will take you directly into Pulichev."

"Yes, I see it now," said the old woman. "Thank you very much, young man. I hope you find the solution to your problems soon. It is unhealthy to live with so much worry."

The old woman headed down the hillside towards the road, and Shloime returned to his seat on the boulder and to his previous thoughts. After a minute or two, he looked up to see if the old woman had found her way to the road, but to his astonishment, she was nowhere in sight.

Shloime jumped to his feet and ran down the hillside. There was no trace of the woman. He ran to the road and looked both ways. Only emptiness as far as he could see. Shaken, Shloime realized that there had been no old woman, that it had all been in his mind.

There could be only one explanation. His prayers had been answered, and he had been given what he had asked. Somewhere in the conversation there lay the key to his dream.

Quickly, he reviewed the conversation in his mind while he could still remember every word. Then, suddenly the answer struck him like a bolt of lightning.

Furiously, he reviewed the events of the past few weeks and all their puzzling aspects. How right Reb Yomtov had been! Things were indeed not always as they seemed. But now it all seemed to fit into place, especially the timing of all that had taken place. It was so simple! Yes, it had to be! It would explain where

Zbigniew Mzlateslavski was hiding and how he had been able to execute the plot.

Shloime was overjoyed. He could already feel the imminent collapse of the plot against the Jews of Pulichev. And he even dared hope that they could soon find the antidote for his mother's mysterious illness. It was as if the sun had suddenly broken through the black clouds that had darkened his life for the past few months.

Another thought struck Shloime. It was not enough for him to know the answers, as he himself had pointed out to his father the previous evening. He had to be able to prove it tomorrow to Jan Bilutsa, but he was confident that he would be able to do so. He had been shown a dream in distant Wielkowicz that had been uncannily accurate, he thought. He had been given the explanation on the eve of the bishop's arrival. All that remained was to find a way to prove it. The *Ribono Shel Olam* would surely show him the solution to this problem as well.

The most promising approach was still the one he had discussed with his father and Elisha the previous evening. The problem was to find a method to extract the information from Kalman Kalb in such a way that the bishop would be convinced. But now that Shloime knew the nature of that information it would be easier to tackle the problem.

It was in quite a confident mood that Shloime set off down the hillside towards Pulichev, turning the problem over and over in his mind as he walked. They will be wondering what happened to me, thought Shloime suddenly, and he quickened his pace. It was midafternoon when he returned home.

There had indeed been some concern in Pulichev about his whereabouts, but Reb Mendel had been sure that he had just gone off to a quiet place where he could think undisturbed. Elisha was waiting outside, nervously pacing back and forth, when Shloime turned into the street.

"Where have you been?" he demanded.

"Elisha, my friend, we have a lot of planning to do," said Shloime. "But first we must make arrangements to travel to

Malonavka tonight and meet with our old friend Jan Bilutsa, the illustrious Bishop of Malonavka."

"What are you talking about?" asked Elisha, giving Shloime an odd look.

"It will all become clear in due time," said Shloime. "We have to make a presentation of evidence before him tomorrow. What I have in mind is a little irregular, so we have to go to Malonavka and prepare Bilutsa for what we plan to do."

"What exactly do we plan to do?"

"We can discuss it on the way. Why don't you go arrange for a wagon and driver, while I have a few words with my father and look in on my mother? Would you mind?"

Reb Mendel was standing in his study deeply immersed in prayer. He looked up when Shloime came in.

"Father!" he exclaimed. "Please sit down. *Baruch Hashem*, I think I have the answers to many of the questions we have. I know where Mzlateslavski is hiding, and I know how he managed to do what he did. We still have to use Kalman Kalb to prove it, but I think I have even discovered how to do that."

"*Baruch Hashem!*" exclaimed Reb Mendel. "Our *tefillos* were answered. Oh, how wonderful! Tell me everything."

"Father, would you trust me?" asked Shloime.

"Of course."

"I cannot tell you what I have discovered. You see, Father, you have a special relationship with Kalman Kalb; you are his support. What I have in mind might be a little painful for him. It is extremely important that he has the security and reassurance of your unqualified support. He will only feel that way if you have no part in what I am doing, if you know nothing at all about it."

Reb Mendel looked at Shloime in bewilderment.

"Can you tell me anything?" he asked.

"You know that I would love to tell you everything, to discuss my plan at length, to hear your comments and suggestions. But it is better that I say nothing. Believe me."

"Shloimele, I trust you," said Reb Mendel. "Just tell me exactly what to do tomorrow, and I shall do it."

"Thank you, Father," said Shloime with relief.

He embraced his father and went up to see his mother. She was awake and glad to see him, but she was pitifully weak. She didn't even have the strength to whisper. She motioned him to bend over and speak directly into her ear.

"Mother," he said. "There is some hope. Please be strong for just a little while longer."

She nodded weakly and dozed off. Shloime was not sure if she had even understood what he had said.

As he left, Kalman Kalb was at his usual post outside the study door. Shloime patted him on the shoulder and smiled at him reassuringly. Kalman Kalb grunted.

Kalman Kalb · 9

EVERYTHING WAS ARRANGED by noon of the following day. The plan had been very carefully formulated down to the most minute detail. Shloime and Elisha had made a quick trip to Malonavka to seek Jan Bilutsa's cooperation. The bishop had been puzzled by Shloime's request but had agreed to cooperate. Reb Mendel had also been cooperative. He had acceded without question to Shloime's request that he keep Kalman Kalb away from the *shul* until noon. Shloime had also asked all the people who normally learned in the *shul* during the daytime to learn elsewhere that day. They had all agreed.

Shloime waited impatiently in the bright sunlight in front of the *shul*. Reb Mendel and Kalman Kalb would be arriving at any moment now. Elisha should also be ready to do his part by now. Shloime hoped that Elisha would not become flustered. This might be their only chance. It was essential that everything go exactly according to plan.

Reb Mendel and Kalman Kalb came into view. Shloime took a deep breath and went forward to meet them.

"Have you been waiting long?" asked Reb Mendel.

"Only a few minutes," Shloime replied.

He took Kalman's hand.

"How are you, Kalman?" he said. "I'm so glad you are here. Come, let's go into the *shul*."

Kalman Kalb responded with his usual grunt.

Coming in from the sunlit street, it took them a moment to adjust to the gloomy darkness inside the *shul*. All the shutters had been closed and the heavy drapes drawn. The only light came from three candles in the center of the *shul* that threw flickering shadows on the walls. There was not a soul in sight. The area in front of the *Aron Hakodesh* had been cleared. Two chairs had been positioned directly in front of the *Aron Hakodesh* but some distance back.

"Father, you can take this chair over here," said Shloime, indicating one of the two chairs. "Kalman, you sit in this other one."

Kalman Kalb remained standing, but Reb Mendel took him gently by the hand, as a father with a small child, and led him to his seat.

"Very good," said Shloime when they were both seated. "Now we can begin."

Shloime walked over to the *Aron Hakodesh* and pulled aside the *paroches*. Then he opened the doors wide.

A five branched candlelabrum had been placed on a little stand in front of the *Aron Hakodesh*. Shloime lit the five candles. Then he walked to the center of the *shul* and extinguished the other three candles. The only light in the *shul* now came from the candelabrum in front of the *Aron Hakodesh*. Most of the *shul* lay shrouded in shadows. Reb Mendel and Kalman Kalb sat in a pool of dim light, their eyes riveted on the gleaming blue, red and white velvet-covered *Sifrei Torah*. Kalman Kalb shivered and held on tightly to Reb Mendel's hand.

"What is the meaning of this, Shloimele?" asked Reb Mendel.

"I beg you, Father," said Shloime. "Please trust me."

Shloime stood facing Kalman Kalb but slightly to the left so as not to obstruct Kalman Kalb's view of the *Aron Hakodesh*. With the only light in the *shul* at his back Shloime appeared as a dark, featureless form.

"Kalman, please listen very carefully to what I am going to tell you," Shloime began in a low, gentle tone. "It is a story about what happened to me when I was a little boy.

"For many years my father and mother had not had any children, and you can imagine their happiness when I was finally born. You know yourself, Kalman, that my parents are both good people. No one is better deserving of a little happiness."

Reb Mendel was staring at Shloime in bewilderment.

"What are you doing, Shloimele?," he said. "You know that he doesn't understand what you are saying to him."

"I understand, Father," said Shloime. "But I think I know how to reach him. I beg you to bear with me."

"Very well, Shloimele," said Reb Mendel in a doubtful voice.

"Kalman," Shloime continued. "My father says that you don't understand what I am saying. But somewhere locked inside you is a soul that *does* hear what I am saying. I am talking to that soul. Please listen very carefully to what I am saying, soul of Kalman Kalb, because only you can help us.

"As I was saying, my parents were wonderfully happy when I was born. But there was a man who lived in Pulichev at that time who could not bear to see the happiness of my parents. He was the local priest. His name was Zbigniew Mzlateslavski.

"Mzlateslavski was a thoroughly evil man. He hated Jews with a passion, but not because we believed differently than he did. No, this man was so full of blind hatred that he could only be happy if he made other people suffer. And the Jews were the perfect target for him. He could persecute them and bring tragedy upon them to his heart's content. And all in the name of the Church. But did he really care for the Church?" Shloime's voice rose sharply. "He most certainly did not! He used the Church to satisfy his own need to destroy, to cause suffering, injury and even death.

"So what did this Mzlateslavski do when he saw how happy my parents were when I was born? He arranged that some bandits should abduct me, and having torn me away from the loving embrace of my parents, he placed me in a convent to be raised as an orphan. Then he returned to his normal life. He was satisfied. He had brought tragedy to my parents, and he had replaced the joy in my own life with misery.

"Years later, Mzlateslavski turned his poisonous attention to the Jews of Krakow. Here was a growing and prosperous community of Jewish people who were assuming an increasingly important role in the entire region. What an inviting target they presented to this most evil man! He spread rumors against them and schemed against them for a long time, until he was finally in a position to destroy this large Jewish community.

"But Hashem would not let him be successful, and when the fateful day came, my father and I were able to thwart his scheme. Mzlateslavski not only failed, he was disgraced. His evil nature was revealed to the whole world. He was an embarrassment to the church, and he was locked away in an old, unused rectory in the monastery at Konstantin. The church wanted to forget this evil creature who had brought it only shame.

"Unfortunately, it was not to be. There was a fire in the rectory, and it burned to the ground. The monks had heard Mzlateslavski screaming from amongst the flames and assumed that he had perished. But he did not perish. He was only injured. Mzlateslavski escaped.

"What do you think was on the mind of this monster when he escaped, dear soul of Kalman Kalb? He wanted revenge. Oh, how he wanted revenge! He always liked to make other people suffer, but now it was worse. He himself was suffering the pain and frustration of utter failure and disgrace. His own life was ruined, and the Jews had returned to a normal life! This could not be! He had to have revenge.

"And against whom do you think he decided to take his revenge? Against my father and my mother! Are there any two kinder people than these two? Who should know better than you, dear soul of Kalman Kalb? But this did not matter to this evil monster, this Mzlateslavski. He came to Pulichev in stealth and began to lay his evil plans from his hiding place, wherever that was.

"First he began with my mother. Somehow he managed to infect her with a mysterious illness from which she suffers to this day. She is wasting away before my father's very eyes, but very, very slowly. She is going to die very soon. You know this better than anyone, soul of Kalman Kalb, since you stand so loyally by my father's side. Can you imagine what unspeakable evil lies in the heart of this Mzlateslavski? Can you imagine a slower and more horrible revenge?

"But wait! It was not enough to punish my father and mother. No! Mzlateslavski had to avenge himself on all the Jews of Pulichev. He appeared at night to his successor as the local priest, a man called Karol Triefak, and to a local troublemaker, a blacksmith called Roman Szczyrk. He convinced these men that he was a messenger from Heaven, and he used them to carry out his plan against the Jews of Pulichev. A blood libel, no less! Mzlateslavski was again showing that he did not care for the Church. The Church is against blood libels. But he is so full of hatred that he doesn't even care if he makes a mockery of his own Church, as long as he can bring destruction and bloodshed to the good Jewish people of Pulichev. He arranged to have a Christian child killed, probably by his henchman Roman Szczyrk. Then he concealed a flask of the child's blood in the *shul* when no one was around. Only you were here, dear Kalman, and he struck you down with a blow to the head.

"What an evil man this is, dear soul of Kalman Kalb! There is no good in this man, only evil. No fine human sentiments, only venom and hatred. This is not a human being, dear soul of Kalman Kalb. It is a monster!"

Shloime paused for breath. Kalman Kalb had grown red in the face. He was trembling violently, what seemed like a growing rage suffused his disfigured face. Reb Mendel was astonished at the effect Shloime's impassioned words were having on Kalman Kalb, but he held his silence. He did not understand what was going on, and he did not want to risk breaking this spell that Shloime had woven.

"What could we do, dear soul of Kalman Kalb? How could we show that we were not responsible for this terrible crime which Mzlateslavski had laid at our doorstep? We had to find where he was hiding. We had to show that he was very much alive and not a messenger from heaven. We had to prove his guilt. But where could we start?

"We had a few small clues. I had had a dream which gave us

some clues. In my dream there was a black shadow who attacked Pulichev. Only I could see it. The other people of Pulichev could only feel its presence, but they couldn't see it. And my father and mother were completely unaware of its presence! Then there was the fact that he never showed his face when he appeared to Karol Triefak. Why was he always so careful to hide his face?

"And there was you, dear Kalman. You probably saw him when he came to hide the blood. But more important, you probably saw him during your evening excursions. We think that you might even know where he is hiding. Not very much, I admit, but that is all we have."

Kalman Kalb had calmed down, but he was still looking intently at Shloime. He did not utter a sound.

"We had no one to turn to but you, dear soul of Kalman Kalb. You were our only hope. But how could we get through to you? How could we reach into that inner chamber where you are confined?

"The only way was through something in your own past life, something that meant very much to you, that would arouse your tortured soul and make it burst forth out of its chains.

"My father told me the little that he knew about you, although he had never told it to anyone else. He told me what he had deduced from the flyleaf of your *Siddur* and what he had learned from a letter that he had written. Now we knew that you were once a mason in Gdryna, we knew the names of the members of your family, we knew about your inheritance, your setting out for Krakow with your family. The rest we could only guess.

"Your family was attacked on the road by bandits. They were all killed and you were mutilated and left for dead. But you were not dead. When you regained consciousness and saw what had happened, when you saw the dead bodies of your wife and children, the pain you felt was too overwhelming to bear. You withdrew into some secret chamber in your mind and remain huddled there until this day. Your outer shell wandered about from town to town, until you finally came to Pulichev. The kindness shown to you by my father and mother touched you, and you stayed.

"Now, dear soul of Kalman Kalb, the time has come when you can repay that kindness."

Shloime paused. Kalman Kalb sat motionless.

"I have prayed, dear soul of Kalman Kalb," Shloime continued. "I have prayed very hard for a way to reach you, and my prayers have been answered."

Shloime moved to the side and pointed towards the *Aron Hakodesh*.

"Look, Kalman! Look closely at the *Aron Hakodesh!* Very few people are privileged to see what we are about to see. And it is only because the Jews of Pulichev are in such great peril that we are being allowed to witness this now."

Shloime turned to face the *Aron Hakodesh*. The candles in the candelabrum had burned down halfway. The *Sifrei Torah* stood as silent witnesses from another world to the scene unfolding before them. Shloime extended both hands towards the *Aron Hakodesh* and closed his eyes. He stood that way for several long moments. When he opened his eyes he seemed to be in a trance.

"This humble human begs to speak with the spirits of the departed," he said in a slow, hollow voice.

Silence.

"I ask this only because the Jewish people of Pulichev are in great peril," he continued in the same dreamlike voice.

There was a very faint sound of stirring in the *Aron Hakodesh*. Suddenly, a distant but surprisingly strong voice rang out.

"Who dares to disturb the spirits of the departed!? Who are you?"

"I am Shloime Pulichever, the son of Reb Mendel Pulichever, the *Rav* of Pulichev."

"Reb Mendel Pulichever is a respected name in this world," said the voice in a friendlier tone. "What do you want?"

"We want to speak with Avraham Kalb of Gdryna, the father of Kalman Kalb."

"Very well. I shall summon Avraham Kalb."

The silence as they waited was deafening. Both of Kalman Kalb's hands were clamped onto Reb Mendel's arm. All eyes were glued to the open doors of the *Aron Hakodesh*.

Suddenly, a white mist appeared between the candelabrum and the *Aron Hakodesh*. It floated upward, the *Sifrei Torah* still faintly visible through the mist. A new and angry voice rang out.

"Who dares to disturb my rest?"

"I am Shloime Pulichever, son of Reb Mendel Pulichever. Are you Avraham Kalb?"

"I am."

"We beg your forgiveness for disturbing you. The Jews of Pulichev are in terrible danger. We think that you may be able to help us."

"I certainly do not mind being summoned if I can help my Jewish brothers anywhere. It is a special privilege to be able to do so after one has already passed on."

"We are very grateful."

"But what can you want of me? Pulichev is all the way in the south, and I was never south of Warsaw. How can I help you?"

"It involves your son Kalman."

"What has my son Kalman to do with it?"

"There is some information that he knows that can help us. But unfortunately, the pain of witnessing the death of his family made him into a mute. We think he will regain his power of speech if you speak to him."

"I don't understand."

"We have brought your son Kalman here." Shloime turned to point at Kalman Kalb. "There he is!"

"That man? He is not my son. My son Kalman has been with me for a long time. The man you have here is not even Jewish."

Reb Mendel and Shloime turned their shocked eyes on Kalman Kalb. Kalman Kalb had shrunk back in terror. They stood frozen this way for what seemed like an eternity. Shloime was the first to break the silence.

"You are not Kalman Kalb!" he shouted, his accusing finger pointing like a dagger. "Poor Kalman Kalb died along with the rest of his family. But I know who you really are.

"Zbigniew Mzlateslavski, that's who you are!

"You were horribly disfigured in the fire at Konstantin. You put on these shabby old clothes, bent over in a deep stoop, walked with a shuffle, carried about that old *Siddur* you had found somewhere, and suddenly, you were Kalman Kalb. Who would recognize the tall, refined Mzlateslavski in this pitiful creature you had become?

"But we should have realized it from the beginning. Why didn't Mzlateslavski show his face to Triefak and Szczyrk? Because they would recognize him as Kalman Kalb; it was unsafe for anyone to know. Why weren't my father and mother aware of the black shadow in the dream? Because the villain was their own Kalman Kalb, whom they had accepted into their hearts. Why did the people of Pulichev only sense the presence of the black shadow without actually seeing it? Because they had become accustomed to seeing Kalman Kalb about. Why was I able to see the black shadow? Because I had been away and did not know Kalman Kalb.

"Yes, Kalman Kalb was the perfect disguise for you. You could roam about at night and no one would pay you any attention. You had entry to the *shul* and to my father's house. You hid the flask here, and then you struck yourself a blow so that no one would suspect you.

"It is you who are the black shadow, Zbigniew Mzlateslavski! You almost succeeded, but once again you failed. We have discovered who you really are. Your plot is uncovered. You have lost, Zbigniew Mzlateslavski."

A transformation was taking place before their eyes. The man they had known as Kalman Kalb was slowly fading away, and a familiar figure was taking his place. He had straightened up to his full height and had assumed the confident posture of a man of the world. The contortion of his features had relaxed somewhat. And he was laughing.

"You poor, miserable Jews," he said in an eerily calm voice. "Do you really think I've lost? Are you going to bring your miserable departed spirit to testify before the bishop against me? Bilutsa may be a fool, but he's not such a fool."

He paused.

"So you think I am a thoroughly evil person?" he continued. "Well, you are wrong. It is you Jews who are thoroughly evil, and I shall have the final laugh. I do not have long to live, did you know that? My heart is very weak. But I shall have the satisfaction of victory before I die. My work here is done. There is no reason for me to remain here. I shall simply disappear and leave you all to the fate that you so richly deserve. And now I shall bid you good day."

"Stay right where you are!" came an authoritative voice from behind a partition.

Pyotr Tambok and several of the count's soldiers emerged. Tambok stationed his considerable bulk in front of the door, while his soldiers went about lighting the darkened lamps of the *shul*. Then Jan Bilutsa, the Bishop of Malonavka, emerged. He was followed by two attendants and Karol Triefak.

All eyes turned to a commotion coming from the direction of the *Aron Hakodesh*. Two hands had appeared from the partial opening of the huge drawer in its bottom, which had become visible in the light of the lamps, and were pulling the drawer open. When it was fully open the tiny figure of Elisha Ringel stepped out. He carried a sack of fine, white powder and was brushing off the powder that had settled onto his clothing when he had blown into the sack.

The sudden realization of how he had been outsmarted and the humiliation of his total defeat hit Mzlateslavski like a physical blow. He let out a piercing, deranged howl. Then he clutched his chest and let out a scream of a different sort. He gasped for breath, as if a giant fist were holding his chest and squeezing it, and slowly crumpled to the ground.

As Mzlateslavski lay there on the ground, his old heart slowly grinding to a halt, his eyes fluttered open. Reb Mendel crouched down on the ground near the dying man.

"Mzlateslavski!" Reb Mendel cried. "Listen to me! You are dying. For you there will be no tomorrow. Let your last deed here on this earth be one of kindness. Take pity on my wife. What has she ever done to you besides showing you kindness? Mzlateslavski! Can you hear me?"

Mzlateslavski opened his mouth to speak, but no words came out.

"Please, please," sobbed Reb Mendel. "I'm begging you. What caused her illness? What will restore her to health? For her sake, please tell me."

Mzlateslavski remained silent, malice gleaming in his eyes. Jan Bilutsa walked over to the dying man and looked down at him.

"Listen to me, Mzlateslavski," said Bilutsa. "You may consider me a fool, but I am still a bishop. If you do not tell the rabbi what he needs to know, I shall excommunicate you right here and now and condemn your miserable soul to eternal damnation. This is your last chance, Mzlateslavski. Make your choice."

Mzlateslavski's eyes were starting to glaze over. His breathing came in a shallow rattle. With a final effort, he managed a hoarse whisper.

"The . . . devil's . . . brew."

Then he died.

The Devil's Brew · 10

THE EXPLANATION OF THE DYING WORDS of Zbigniew Mzlateslavski came from a most unexpected quarter. Karol Triefak knocked on the door shortly after Jan Bilutsa returned to Malonavka and asked to speak to Reb Mendel. Reb Mendel welcomed him cordially, ushered him into the study and offered him some freshly brewed tea and a plate of biscuits. Shloime and Elisha joined them.

"I have to tell you, Rabbi," Triefak said when he had relaxed a bit, "that I feel terrible about this whole affair. By now, all of Pulichev has learned the truth, and Roman Szczyrk, who was surely guilty of killing that poor child, has conveniently disappeared. You know, we have always had peaceful relations with the Jews of Pulichev. I hope we can continue to do so in spite of what has happened."

"I hope so, too," said Reb Mendel.

"Actually, the reason I came is to tell you something I suddenly remembered. You know, when old Mzlateslavski mentioned the devil's brew it sounded a little familiar. But I couldn't recall where I had heard those words."

He paused to sip his tea. Reb Mendel and Shloime sat on the edges of their chairs hanging on his every word. Triefak wiped his lips and continued.

"The devil's brew was a potion used by some of the old peasants of the Dukla region, high up in the Carpathian Mountains," he explained. "My grandparents lived in a small village in that region. We used to visit them there sometimes. I used to enjoy those visits very much. But we didn't go very often, of course. It was too hard for my parents to travel with all the children, and besides, we didn't have much money. My grandparents never visited us. Never. You know —"

Shloime's cough had interrupted Triefak's rambling. Reb Mendel took advantage of the momentary pause.

"You were telling us about the devil's brew," prompted Reb Mendel.

"Ah yes, of course," said Triefak, regaining his train of thought. "It was my grandmother who mentioned it. Sometimes, when I was annoying her, she would threaten to feed me the devil's brew. I asked her what it was, but she didn't want to tell me. I found out anyway."

He paused again to sip his tea.

"It seems that the devil's brew is a mixture of many things," he continued after wiping his lips. "It was used to cause a slow, painful death to one's enemies. But it could also be used to punish them without killing them. The mixture could only kill if it was fed to the victim for a very long time. If he stopped taking it he would recover. Unless he was too far gone, of course. It was really quite a devilish brew."

Apparently finished, Triefak turned his undivided attention to his tea.

"Do you know how was this devil's brew administered?" asked Shloime.

"That was the hard part," replied Triefak. "It had to be given almost daily. The person who administered it had to be fairly close to the victim."

"Do you know any of the ingredients of this devil's brew?" asked Shloime.

"Not all of them," said Triefak. "I know that there were some herbs in it that helped the victim stay alive. And the main ingredient was a poison. Arsenic, I think."

Reb Mendel bolted out of his chair.

"The porridge!" he exclaimed as he ran out of the room, Shloime close on his heels.

They bounded up the stairs and into the Rebbetzin's room. She was asleep, her breathing barely audible. The jar of porridge stood on the table in its usual place. It was half empty.

Shloime picked up the jar gingerly and carried it down the stairs to the kitchen. He then prepared a bowl of fresh porridge for his mother.

"It must have been quite easy for Mzlateslavski," said Reb Mendel to Shloime and Elisha as they sat together in the study a short while later. "He must have had many opportunities to slip the poison into the porridge while it was being prepared in the kitchen. No one ever paid him any attention. Tell us, Shloime, what made you suspect Kalman Kalb?"

"I take very little credit for that, Father," said Shloime and went on to tell him about the old woman on the hillside. "When I realized that she was bringing me a message it struck me. When I stood up she expressed her surprise that I was tall since I had looked quite short sitting there on the boulder, hunched over with my head in my hands. It was then that I realized that although Kalman Kalb was a large man he could be considered short because he was so hunched over. Once I started to consider Kalman Kalb everything fell into place."

"Truly amazing," said Reb Mendel. "We have to thank the *Ribono Shel Olam.*"

"I have one question," said Elisha. "If Shloime had been sent a warning through his dream, why did it have to be so cryptic, so difficult to decipher? Why couldn't the message have been simple and clear?"

"An excellent question, Elisha," said Reb Mendel. "But tell me, if the message had been clear would all of us have *davened* to the *Ribono Shel Olam* as fervently as we did?"

"No, I suppose not," admitted Elisha.

"Then there is the answer to your question."

Over the next few weeks the Rebbetzin slowly recovered her strength, and Pulichev breathed a sigh of relief. Reb Mendel and Shloime took turns caring for her. Bracha Surkis came by to help as often as she could, and the neighbors were very helpful as well. Reb Asher Sofer came over often from Molodietz to visit his convalescing sister and to spend some time with his daughter Bracha and his grandchildren.

As *Pesach* approached, the Rebbetzin's recovery quickened. She become stronger by the day as her system cleansed itself of the poison it had absorbed.

Pesach that year was a bittersweet time in Reb Mendel's household. Bracha Surkis and her children came to the *Sedarim*, as well as Elisha Ringel, who had stayed on for a while. The Rebbetzin's steady recovery was a cause for rejoicing, but the memory of the death of Ephraim Surkis *al Kiddush Hashem* tinged everything with a touch of sadness.

Glossary of Terms

Glossary of Terms

(Terms are in Hebrew unless otherwise indicated.)

al Kiddush Hashem: to sanctify the Name

amud: cantor's lectern

Aron Hakodesh: Holy Ark containing Torah scrolls

Ay: expression of lament [Yiddish]

Bais Hamikdash: the Holy Temple in Jerusalem

Baruch Hashem: blessed is the Name

bitachon: trust

Chumash: the Five Books of Moses

daven(ed)(ing): pray(ed)(ing)

drash(ah)(os): sermon(s)

Gan Eden: the Garden of Eden, paradise

Gemara: Amoraic part of the Talmud

goyische: gentile [Yiddish]

Halachic: pertaining to Torah law

Havdalah: ritual marking the end of *Shabbos*

hesped: eulogy

Kabbalas Shabbos: liturgical welcome to *Shabbos*

Kedushah: the third blessing of the *Shemoneh Esray*

Lechah Dodi: part of *Kabbalas Shabbos*

lichtige: illuminated [Yiddish]

Maariv: evening prayer service

matzos: unleaven bread

melamed: teacher

Minchah: afternoon prayer service

minyan: quorum of ten for prayer

Mishnayos: Tanaic part of the Talmud

mitzv(ah)(os): commandment(s)

nachas: pleasure of fulfillment

paroches: drape of the *Aron Hakodesh*

Pesach: Festival of Passover

Rabbosai: gentlemen

Rav (Rabbonim): rabbi(s)

Reb Yid: Mr. Jew, sir [Yiddish]

Rebbe: master, teacher

refuah shelaimah: complete recovery

Ribono Shel Olam: Master of the Universe

Sedarim: elaborate ceremonial *Pesach* feast

sefarim: books

Sefer (Sifrei) Torah: Torah
scroll(s)
Shabbos: Sabbath
Shacharis: morning prayer
service
Shalom Aleichem: peace to
you, greetings
Shemoneh Esray: the
Eighteen Blessings prayer
shiur(im): lecture(s)
Shiva: seven-day period of
formal mourning
shul(s): synagogue(s)

Siddur: prayer book
tallis: prayer shawl
Talmid Chacham: Torah
scholar
tefillin: phylacteries
tefill(ah)(os): prayer(s)
Tehillim: Book of Psalms
Tikun Chatzos: Midnight
Lamentations
tzaddik: righteous
person
Yom Tov: Festival
zchus: privilege

The Ruach Ami Series

traces the spellbinding saga of the fictional Pulichever family from the early part of the seventeenth century in the Kingdom of Poland. It is rich in historical information, Torah values and literary content. Six volumes of this exciting saga are available, with at least six more in preparation.

The Promised Child

Reb Mendel and Sarah Pulichever embark on a journey to Krakow, setting off a long chain of events that reach a startling climax over thirty years later. A gripping story of heartbreak, hope and spine-tingling suspense.

Two completely new chapters and a wealth of historical information have been added to the revised and expanded edition.

The Dream

Shloime Pulichever returns home to find his mother suffering from a mysterious illness and a dangerous phantom lurking in the shadows of Pulichev. The story takes place in a time of peace and prosperity for the Jews of Poland, but the cold winds of change are already in the air.

The Year of the Sword

The Pulichever family suffers through the devastating pogroms of Bogdan Chmielnicki and his Cossack hordes during the Ukranian uprising of 5408 (1648), the terrible year of *Tach*. An inspiring story of danger, courage and unshakable faith.

Twilight

Reb Shloime and Bracha Pulichever travel to Warsaw for the wedding of their son Ahrele, but unexpected complications arise. A story of people trying to bind up their wounds and build for the future once again.

The Impostor

The characters of the Pulichever saga meet the false *Mashiach* Shabbesai Tzvi. This amazing story follows Shabbesai Tzvi's movement from its origins with mysterious midnight meetings to its hair-raising climax in the Imperial palace of the Turkish Sultan.

The Purple Ring

The Purple Ring revolves around a secret conspiracy to discredit the Jewish townspeople of the fictional city of Pulichever and accuse them of high treason. There are many sinister developments as the exciting story unfolds, including captured Turkish spies, teams of assassins and plots within plots hatched under the dark midnight skies.